CW00506508

Horror Legends Unleashed

Horror Legends Unleashed, Volume 1

The Craptitude

Published by Craptitude Publications, 2023.

HORROR LEGENDS UNLEASHED

First edition. October 21, 2023.

Copyright © 2023 The Craptitude.

ISBN: 979-8215677889

Written by The Craptitude.

Table of Contents

To all the horror enthusiasts out there,

This book is dedicated to those who love to be terrified, who revel in the thrill of the unknown, and who can't resist a good scare. It's for those who have stayed up late reading horror novels under the covers, or who have binged on horror movies until the early hours of the morning.

But most of all, this book is dedicated to those who have made horror a part of their lives, who have embraced the macabre and the sinister, and who have found comfort in the darkness.

We dedicate these chilling tales to you, our fellow horror lovers, and we hope that they will keep you on the edge of your seat, send shivers down your spine, and haunt your dreams long after you've finished reading.

So turn off the lights, grab a blanket, and prepare to be terrified. We hope you enjoy the journey into the depths of horror that awaits you within these pages.

Yours in terror,

The Craptitude

PS: Lots of Love to my Dear SS

Monsters are real, and ghosts are real too. They live inside us, and sometimes, they win.

Stephen King

Introduction

"Horror Legends Unleashed: Volume 1" beckons you to embark on a chilling journey into the darkest realms of the human imagination. This spine-tingling collection features 25 short stories, each offering a terrifying encounter with the most sinister creatures from the world of horror. From classic monsters to vengeful spirits, witches, and demons, these tales venture into the abyss of fear, promising to awaken your deepest terrors.

Within these pages, readers will confront a legion of horror legends, including the bloodthirsty Chupacabra, the vengeful Kuchisake Onna, and the ever-elusive Jersey Devil. Each story unveils the sinister backstories and motivations that drive these malevolent entities to sow fear and chaos among the unsuspecting.

Set across diverse time periods and locales, from ancient European forests to contemporary American cities, these tales span the breadth of the horror genre. Whether you seek supernatural encounters, psychological torment, or grotesque monstrosities, "Horror Legends Unleashed" has something to offer every aficionado of the macabre.

With 25 distinctive narratives to choose from, readers can dive into this compendium of terror at any point, confident that an unsettling tale awaits them. But fear not, for amidst the darkness, you'll also discover a touch of humor to provide respite from the relentless onslaught of fear. "Horror Legends Unleashed: Volume 1" invites you to confront your most profound fears, navigate the twisted corridors of human creativity, and witness the malevolent entities that lurk just beyond the veil of our reality. Prepare for a journey into the realm of nightmares, where horror knows no bounds.

Chupacabra

O nce upon a time, there was a small village nestled in the mountains of Latin America. The village rested in a valley with a river running through it and farm lands surrounding the village. The terrain was mountainous with many craggy rocks and a few trees.

The villagers lived simple, peaceful lives. They worked their land, tending to their crops and animals in the surrounding fields. During harvest season they would gather together to celebrate the bounty of their labor with food and music. The villagers were also close knit, and rarely ventured beyond the borders of their community, content to remain in the security of their valley home.

Members of the village held a deep respect for nature, believing that all creatures had a place in the natural order of things. Whenever possible, they used natural resources carefully and responsibly to ensure that the environment stayed unspoiled.

It was not unknown for visitors from outside villages to come through from time to time but these travelers were usually welcomed with open arms as long as they were respectful and followed the village's codes of conduct. Unfortunately, this also meant that occasionally outsiders would bring problems into the village with them—from petty theft to more serious offenses like poaching or illegal logging. Whenever such issues arose, it was up to a council of elders who lived in and around the village to decide how best to handle conflicts between locals and outsiders alike.

One day, however, a strange creature appeared in their midst, unlike they had never seen before. And this was no ordinary traveler. The creature stood on its hind legs, its body flattened like a lizard, it's spine covered in spines similar to a porcupine. It had long pointy ears and the tips of his spines glinted in the sunlight. The creature's eyes were large and red. It stood on its four legs, with a long tail dragging behind it. It looked like a bear, but it had red eyes, claws and two pairs of fangs. The creature's body reeked of the wet, musky odor of the forest floor.

Despite the harsh summer day and the piercing sunlight, its face was like a shadow and its eyes glinted like two red pins in the darkness. It was like a black shadow had come to life, a creature made of hellfire, holding a knife from a nightmare.

The villagers were both fearful and curious of the strange creature. They had never seen anything like it before and wondered what it wanted. One brave villager stepped forward and cautiously approached the creature, asking if it needed help. The creature slowly raised its head and looked directly at the villager with its piercing red eyes. Then, without warning, it leapt up onto a nearby goat and began to eat it.

The villagers were horrified as they watched the creature devour the poor animal in front of them. They shouted for it to leave but their pleas fell on deaf ears. With a few swift movements, the creature finished consuming its meal and then turned its gaze back towards the village, completely unperturbed by their cries of protest.

The villagers stood frozen in fear as they pondered what to do next. Suddenly one of them remembered that there was an old legend about a demon-like creature, the Chupacabra that lurked in these mountains and fed off other living creatures. Could this be that same beast?

Just as they were getting ready to march towards the menacing figure, it suddenly disappeared into thin air without a trace. All that remained was a pool of blood where the poor goat had been feasted upon moments before.

The villagers were terrified, for they had never seen anything like it before. The creature looked nothing like the small, furry animals that lurked in woods and gave them such good sport with their bows and arrows. The dark shape was more than twice as tall as a man, slinking about on its long legs, skittering here and there on four paws that ended in wicked claws. It seemed to be stalking something or someone, remaining unnaturally still at first, then pouncing forward and devouring its prey.

The villagers tried to set traps for it; lights were placed outside of homes and livestock pens so that they could see where it went at night. But it was too quick and elusive, always managing to evade their grasp. As the weeks passed, the villagers grew increasingly desperate. The creature quickly gained a reputation for attacking and drinking the blood of their livestock, particularly goats and sheep.

The Legend of the Chupacabra spread like wildfire. The children in the village had nightmares of drinking the blood of their goats when they grew up so that they could become huge black monsters. The villagers feared for their livelihoods and their safety, and they knew that they needed to find a way to get rid of the creature once and for all.

In the village, there lived a young girl named Esperanza. Esperanza, who was just seventeen years old, her waist-length hair was the color of a raven's wing, the tips burning a brilliant red like fire. Her eyes were like pools of crystal clear water. Her skin, the color of mocha. She had a brilliant smile, and a fetching personality. Her laughter was like the tinkling of bells.

As the first drops of rain pelted the dry, cracked earth, after a draught that lasted years, she came into this world. The long-awaited relief from the unyielding heat and dust, a sign of new beginnings in the arid village. Because of her timely arrival, many of the villagers considered her to be an omen of good luck and began to look to her for guidance and advice even though she was just a teenager. Her parents died when she was just five and the whole village cared for her like she was their own daughter itself.

Esperanza had heard the stories about the Chupacabra but had never seen it. She knew that something needed to be done, but she wasn't sure what could be done since it seemed as if this creature could not be scared or tamed. She decided to consult with some of the wise elders in her village who had knowledge and experience with dealing with such creatures.

The elders advised Esperanza that they must capture the Chupacabra dead or alive and bring it before their god, Huitzilopochtli. Huitzilopochtli was their village deity, a large serpent God, red with black spots. He had three blue eyes and a forked tongue. The markings on his body looked like feathers, and he had large wings. The statue in the village square was fashioned from green stone, and was cast from the mold of Huitzilopochtli's face, though it depicted the god with only one fang instead of two, and lacked the branding scar on his cheek.

They told her that only then would they be able to understand why it was terrorizing their village and put an end to its evil deeds once and for all.

Esperanza set off into the hills with a few villagers in tow. They each carried wooden stakes which, when thrust into its heart, would be enough to stop the Chupacabra forever. Over the next days, they tracked its moves across the forests and mountainsides. Finally, they found the Chupacabra. The creature was lying in the middle of a rock pile. Its lips were parted slightly and they could see the sharp fangs in its mouth. Its eyes were closed, as if sleeping. The villagers crept forward slowly, their feet shuffling over the dirt. Anxiety and wonder filled the air as they drew nearer to the rocky outcropping. In the pale moonlight they could see a strange creature nestled between two stones. Its fur was an oily black and its long spines shimmered in the moonlight — it was the mythical Chupacabra, sleeping soundly.

"Are you sure this is the right creature?" one of the villagers asked Esperanza. "I'm positive," she replied. "I've seen the wounds on the animals. This is the Chupacabra."

The villagers cautiously approached the creature, their weapons at the ready. Esperanza held her breath as they moved closer. One of the villagers reached out and touched it with his spear, causing the Chupacabra to stir briefly before settling back into sleep. It was then that they noticed its eyes were glowing a faint yellow.

Esperanza could feel her heart beating in her chest as she readied herself for what would come next. She had heard stories about how powerful this creature was and was prepared for anything it might throw at them. She took a deep breath and gave a nod to the other villagers. On her signal, they lunged forward, staking it through its heart with their spears.

The Chupacabra screamed in rage and pain as it struggled against the stakes that held it in place. It seemed that no matter how hard it fought, it couldn't break free from their grasp. Finally, after several long minutes, its struggles ceased and its eyes grew dim as its life force left its body forever. The villagers had done it – they had captured the Chupacabra!

Esperanza felt an immense sense of accomplishment as she looked upon the dead creature before her. But now came the hard part – getting it back to their village so that Huitzilopochtli could judge whether or not this creature was truly responsible for all of the destruction in their area.

One of the villagers suggested they use vines to tie up its body so that it could be dragged behind them on their journey back home without causing any more damage or exhaustion than necessary. Although none of them relished carrying such a weighty burden all night long, there was no other choice but to do what must be done if they were going to get justice for their people once and for all!

But as they drew closer, the Chupacabra suddenly sprang to life. It let out a piercing shriek, like a steam pipe bursting on a cold winter night. The Chupacabra's eyes glowed an evil red. The dust rose up around the Chupacabra's feet, mixed with the smoke of grinding stone and the haze of fear.

The beast lunged at the villagers, its fangs bared and its claws extended. The villagers scattered, their weapons clattering to the ground as they tried to evade the creature's attacks. Two were swallowed by the beast, but the third was able to grab his spear and drive it deep into the shoulder of one of the monstrous heads.

Esperanza faced the Chupacabra with a bravery that shook the very ground beneath her feet. Her heart thudded against her chest and raw power surged through her veins as she lunged forward, driving her stake into the creature's chest. A deafening shriek erupted from its throat and Esperanza was sprayed with a shower of blood, each droplet seeming to ignite a fire within her. The Chupacabra leaned in close, sniffing her face intensely before sinking its fangs into her nose. Pain exploded through her skull like wildfire and Esperanza tried to scream, yet nothing came out but an agonizing gasp. As she collapsed onto the ground, time itself seemed to stop as the villagers watched in horror as the Chupacabra turned on them, ready to devour them all.

The villagers stumbled over each other in a desperate attempt to flee the blood-soaked battlefield. As the Chupacabra leapt from victim to victim, Esperanza lay motionless on the ground, her life ebbing away with each passing second.

Finally, the beast was distracted enough for some of the villagers to make it back to their village alive. They ran as quickly as they could and soon found themselves safe and sound in their homes.

Once there, they all gathered around and began discussing what they had seen and experienced. For a while, no one spoke – their minds were still processing the horror of what they had seen and done. But eventually, someone mustered up enough courage to suggest that they go back out and retrieve Esperanza's body so that she could receive her due respects.

At dawn the next day, a small group of brave volunteers arrived at the scene. The Chupacabra was nowhere to be seen. But it was clear that Esperanza was gone from this world; however, many of her possessions remained onsite - her stake which had pierced through its heart, some stones that had been carved with symbols of protection against evil spirits, and even some jewelry which seemed to have been made specially just for her. The villagers collected these items as mementos of her bravery in her fight against this monstrous creature.

So it was that day that Esperanza's body was taken back home in a grand parade fit for a queen - but despite this somber yet beautiful ceremony there were still tears shed by all those who followed behind carrying torches,

And the legend of the Chupacabra lived on, a cautionary tale of the dangers that lurked in the mountains and forests of Latin America, and the price that a young girl paid in the pursuit of trying to vanquish the dreaded Chupacabra.

$$\Delta\Delta\Delta$$

La Llorona

"It's getting late, Abuela. Shouldn't we head back?" asked young Maria, as she looked out at the darkening river. The river was as dark as night, as if a cloud of black ink had floated down the river and was spreading across the water. Dark and eddying, a coil of black water broken by a stripe of sun struggling at the shoreline. There was a canopy of leaves above, and the afternoon light was fading.

The sun still shone, its rays piercing the water's surface and igniting the river's ripples into fiery sparks. The moon was rising, its silver light reflecting off the water danced along its ripples. The forest beyond the water looked to be warped and twisted, the trees twisted into hags and demons beyond the river's edge.

Maria was a tiny girl with waist-length brown hair and sandy brown eyes. She was wearing a dark green dress with pink trim. She also had a pair of white, lacy socks covering her feet. She dipped a finger in the water and tasted it. The taste was of the smoky air and red dirt, mixed with the damp moss that grew on the deep banks.

The air smelled of the crisp clean smell of a country evening. Breaths of fresh air that smelled of fireflies and moths just past the light. The crickets chirping, the wind rustling the trees. Fireflies flitting through the air. The whisper of water lapping at the riverbank.

Maria was touching her grandmother's arm, feeling the fabric of her dress. The grass was cool, the dirt was warm and soft beneath her feet. The river was cool as she dipped a toe in.

"No, no, mi niña. We have plenty of time," replied her grandmother with a reassuring smile. "Besides, it's a beautiful night for a walk." Her grandmother's back was hunched over and her grey hair was pinned in a bun. She wore a simple green dress with a violet blouse. Her face was wrinkled and her skin was pale. She moved clumsily, her voice was raspy and her hands shook, but when she laughed it was like a silver bell ringing.

Maria sighed and followed her grandmother along the riverbank. She couldn't shake the feeling that they were being watched, and the sound of the river seemed to echo with whispers that she couldn't quite make out. As they rounded the bend of the river, Maria's breath caught in her throat as she saw a ghostly figure standing on the opposite shore. Dressed head to toe in white, her long black hair fanned out around her like a raven's wings and her eyes shone with an eerie light.

"Who is that, Abuela?" Maria whispered, her voice shaking. "That is La Llorona," her grandmother answered in a low, fearful tone. "She is the spirit of a woman who drowned her children in this river many years ago. She wanders these banks night after night, desperately searching for their lost souls."

Maria shuddered and grasped tightly onto her grandmother's arm. "Why does she do that?" "Because she can never atone for what she has done, and will be cursed to roam these lands until she finds them and lays them to rest."

As they watched, La Llorona began to wail, a stirring sound that tugged at the gut. Maria felt the need to turn and run but knew she must not break eye contact. "Stay calm, mi niña," her grandmother said softly. "She cannot harm us if we do not interfere with her search." The wails grew louder as La Llorona moved farther down the street, her white dress soaked from crying. She turned and followed their path down the sidewalk, stopping when she reached the corner of their yard.

La Llorona wore an expression of regret and sorrow on her face, and her body appeared translucent. She could now see La Llorona moving closer, her eyes fixed on them with a terrifying intensity. Her eyes looked like they were on fire, but they were ice cold. Maria looked away and tried to think of something else. Anything but that face. That horrible, horrible face. The woman's white dress was splattered with blood. Her long black hair swirled around her like a vortex of snakes. Her brows furrowed in a mask of anger and sorrow.

Suddenly, the wailing stopped, and La Llorona disappeared into the mist that was rising from the river. Maria breathed a sigh of relief and turned to her grandmother. "Let's go back, Abuela. I don't want to stay here any longer."

Her grandmother nodded, and they turned to head back along the riverbank. But as they walked away, Maria saw a figure standing on the opposite bank once more. Long hair hung in disheveled strings around its face, and rags floated around its waste as if it were underwater. A red slash cut across one cheek and through the corner of one eye.

It was La Llorona's ghostly figure, and she stared at them with an imploring gaze that held a note of desperation. "Abuela," Maria asked, her voice shaking. "Do you see that woman?" Her grandmother replied, a little angrily "Yes, mi niña. As I told you. she is still searching for her children. And she will continue to do so until she finds them."

Maria quickened her pace, eager to escape the ghostly presence that haunted the riverbank. But as they walked further and further away, Maria had a feeling that they were still near the river. She couldn't shake the feeling, no matter how much she tried to distract herself with thoughts of something else. "Abuela," she said finally, her voice shaking slightly, "why are we still so close to the river? It seems like we have been walking for quite a long time." Her grandmother smiled and put an arm around her shoulders. "Do not worry, mi niña. We will reach our destination soon enough — just keep your pace up." Maria nodded, but despite her efforts to remain calm, she still felt a growing sense of dread in her chest as they continued down the path.

The trees shifted around them in an eerie dance as the wind blew through their leaves. The sun had begun to set and shadows began to creep up from the ground below as they walked further and further away from the safety of their home. Despite this chill air of danger, they kept trekking through until finally they reached a clearing on the edge of town.

Maria looked around in confusion before realizing that it was La Llorona's graveyard. The grass grew tall around them and tombstones poked out among clusters of trees — some so old that the writing had worn away with years of neglect.

Her grandmother took her hand and gave her a solemn look before leading her into the graveyard towards two small stone figures standing side-by-side atop one grave marker — both with names etched into them: Juan and Maria. They were La Llorona's lost children. Tears began streaming down Maria's face, understanding now why La Llorona had been searching for them all these years — it was because she wanted nothing more than to be reunited with them in death just as she could not do in life.

Suddenly, her grandmother stopped, took Maria in her arms and whispered, "Mi hijos... mi hijos..." Maria screamed as her grandmother suddenly transformed into La Llorona in front of her. The spirit's red eyes glowed fiercely in the fading light, and she reached out for Maria with long pale hands. "Mi hijos," La Llorona said in a soft voice, "I have been searching for you for so long."

The tears began to flow down Maria's cheeks as she was pulled closer and closer to the spirit; it felt like an eternity before they were face-to-face, only separated by a few inches. La Llorona placed a finger on Maria's open mouth, silencing her cries and whispering, "Do not be afraid, mi hijos. I will never let go of you. Dont be a bad girl, Mi hijos..." She held Maria tight, "I will never let go, Mi hijos..." and the spirit jumped into the river and disappeared beneath its murky depths taking Maria along with her into the depths of hell.

ΔΔΔ

Kuchisake Onna

The street was lined with cherry blossom trees of pink and white. In the distance, the lights from the Takasaki Shrine cast a yellow haze in the sky. The stones of the shrine were as smooth and moss-covered as a frog's back.

Takasaki was a quiet city. There were street lights and traffic lights, but they were dim and the streets were barren. The air was thick with the aroma of slow-roasted pork and grilled sausages. It smelt of rain. It was a summer shower, but the rain had cleared the streets and lit up the town with a fresh scent of clean air. It smelt of summer's end. The air was fresh, like rain-soaked dirt and wet metal.

A group of teenage girls shared a stick of yakitori, taking turns to eat the meat from the skewer after each bite, tasting only the salt and soy sauce. The walls of the city were covered in graffiti, thick black and red ink, pictures of demons and blood-splattered symbols that no one could recognize. It stank of piss and puke and rotten meat, like the gutters of a city at the height of summer.

It was a place distantly, like a jungle primeval. It was a place that was haunted, that could be drenched with the sweat of fear, that could be branched off with unexpected turnings, that could be shut off in like a box, that could be large or small, that could be near or far, that could be strangely shaped and that could be filled with things obviously other, that could be lovely or horrible, that could be lit with a light that was as bright as any light and that could be covered with darkness so heavy that it was all but tangible, that could be a place where one might cry out in rage, that could be a place where one might sob in despair, that could be alive and teeming, that could be utterly without pity, that could be without grace, that could be so bizarre that nothing in the wildest imagination would ever be able to conjure up anything like it.

In this quiet weird town of Takasaki, there was a legend that sent shivers down the spines of even the bravest of men. The legend of Kuchisake Onna - the woman with the slit mouth. It was said that Kuchisake Onna would roam the streets at night, her face covered by a surgical mask. She would approach unsuspecting victims and ask them a simple question: "Am I pretty?" If the victim answered yes, she would remove her surgical mask, revealing a lacerated, gaping mouth. The wound stretched from ear to ear, revealing muscle and bone on one side. Her bottom lip was missing, her top lip split into one large lip and one small one. She wore a tortured smile on her face. Her eyes were wide, her forehead crinkled with concern.

She would then ask the victim again: "Now, am I pretty?" If the victim answered no, Kuchisake Onna would produce a pair of scissors and cut them open from ear to ear, just like her own disfigured mouth.

But a long long time ago, Kuchisake Onna was beautiful, her skin, smooth like satin or flowing water. Her eyes were the color of the sky on a cloudless day. Her hair, the color of the sun, golden and radiant. She had a wide, toothy smile and long, Her eyes were warm and inviting, almost haunting in their tenderness.

Once, Kuchisake Onna's voice was alluring, like the sound of a violin. It took your breath away with each sweeping note, the sound of wind chimes and the voice of the sea. But now her voice was stained with vengeance, dripping with the blood of her victims. She sounded like a mixture of a whisper and a scream, an echo of someone else's scream.

A life-sized paper doll of her mouth was standing in the middle of a street in Takasaki. The mouth matched her face, and had a small tongue, and very large teeth, and a red gash of a dress, and knee-high boots trimmed in white lace, and a red and white striped sash that went around her middle. The mouth had many small eyes, one for every tooth. The mouth opened wide. It had a large tongue, with many chambers, like a complex worm or coral, and long fang-like teeth that were folded back, and retractable and solid and strong, and a mouthpiece that was large and semi-rigid, and had a small smile on it, that belonged to the mouth. The mouth had small clusters of eye-like spots, on long pink stalks.

On such a summer evening, a group of friends were walking home from a late-night movie. It was already three in the morning. They were laughing and talking loudly, as was their wont. They were singing silly songs and shouting out the punchlines for each other. They were being rowdy and noisy. No one was thinking about what might be lurking in the dark. They were the kind of friends who were always together. Strong ties, through thick and thin. The sort of friends who shared anything and everything with one another. The sort of friends who would stand by their friends even when they were wrong, even when they had done something horrible. Even when they had done something they would regret for the rest of their lives.

The four of them were inseparable. They walked everywhere together, went away on holiday together. They were a giant ball of laughter, rolling along the street, pushing and shoving and knocking into anyone in their way.

One of them was called Tomoko. She was the most naturally beautiful girl in their class. She had the kind of beauty that would steal the hearts of all the boys in the class and even some girls. Roki and Tinaka were the boys, loud and brash. Both had huge crushes on Tomoko but they were too proud to admit it. Rimi was the nerd of the group, always helping the others with their notes and study materials. And secretly, she had a crush on Tomoko as well.

The city was like a graveyard, dark and still. They walked along a quiet street lined with cherry blossom trees of pink and white. In the distance, the lights from the Takasaki Shrine cast a yellow haze in the sky.

The noise of a passing car turned their heads. The street was lit up like a stage. They looked at the car as it slowed down, and drove up the street. The car moved off again, and the group turned to look at each other and relaxed.

As they reached the crossroads near the train station, they found the Kuchisake Onna's doll, still and silent on the pavement, blocking their path. Like a dead animal, it looked like it had been hit by a car. The friends stood and stared at its mouth, half in fear, half in fascination. Roki and Tinoka took pictures on their phones. Tomoko stayed back and hesitantly took a few steps forward. Rimi took out her phone and snapped pictures of the mouth from a safe distance.

It was like a prop from a horror movie, a prop that had ended up in the wrong place. The mouth, like a dead fish, lying there in the middle of the street, blood running from its lips, its tongue curled up in the gutters and mud of the street, the tongue beaten and bitten by the teeth of the passers-by, its teeth broken and split.

Roki and his friends were about to turn their heads back, when a sinister voice cut through the silence - "Am I pretty?" Kuchisake Onna had appeared out of nowhere. The friends were immobilized in fear as she approached them, her face hidden behind her mouthpiece and her chilling gaze stealing the life out of them. Roki uttered a trembling question, "What do you want?". But deep down he knew that when it came to Kuchisake Onna, there was never an answer that would satisfy her hunger. Onna's face was concealed by her veil and her eyes were like blades that stabbed at them with an intense hatred. Fear coursed through their veins as they stood petrified in terror.

"Am I pretty?" she repeated.

No one answered. They just stared in horror at the monster standing before them, its mouth dripping with blood and a wicked smile playing on its lips. After what felt like an eternity of silence, Roki finally mustered up the courage to answer "Yes".

Kuchisake Onna removed her mask, revealing the gruesome

wound that marred her face. "Now, am I pretty?" she asked again, her voice becoming more urgent. The friends hesitated, unsure of what to say. But before they could answer, Kuchisake Onna lunged forward, brandishing a pair of sharp scissors.

"Yes! You are beautiful", Tomoko said calmly. Kuchisake Onna's face twisted into a haunting smile, and the group knew that their lives were in danger. The friends began to run, but it was too late. Kuchisake Onna had already caught up to them and had grabbed hold of Tomoko. It threw her on the ground and started slashing at her face with its scissor-like mouth. The friends screamed as they watched Tomoko desperately trying to get away from the monster.

Roki, Tinaka and Rimi ran for their lives, looking back every now and then to catch a glimpse of what was happening to Tomoko behind them. When they finally reached safety, they realised that Tomoko was no longer with them anymore. She had been captured by Kuchisake Onna and killed in cold blood.

The friends were devastated. They couldn't believe that Tomoko was gone, and they all blamed themselves for not being able to save her. Days passed, and the pain of losing their friend never seemed to go away.

But one day, something miraculous happened - Tomoko returned. The three friends could hardly believe their eyes as their beloved friend walked up to them with a smile on her face, seemingly unchanged by the ordeal she had been through with Kuchisake Onna. She explained that after the monster had captured her and attempted to kill her, she had awoken in a meadow surrounded by beautiful flowers and butterflies. After several days of searching for an escape route, she finally found one and managed to make it back home safely.

Roki, Tinaka and Rimi were filled with joy as they welcomed Tomoko home. But soon enough they started noticing something strange about her - whenever someone asked her if she was ok or if there was anything wrong she would answer with a cryptic smile and her eyes seemed to glint in an unusual way.

The three friends were discussing about Tomoko's wierd behaviour one day. Suddenly, Tomoko appeared out of thin air. The friends screamed in terror as Tomoko emerged from the shadows brandishing a pair of rusty scissors. An eerie calmness seemed to flow through her body, like she was possessed and had been taken over by some unknown force. Her lips twitched in a sinister smirk as she snarled "Am I pretty now?". Her cold eyes locked onto each friend one by one, daring them to make a move. Before they could react, Tomoko lunged forward with frightening speed. The scissors glinted menacingly in the moonlight as she slashed at them with inhuman strength. Chunks of hair and flesh filled the air as screams echoed into the night sky. One by one the terrified friends were cut down mercilessly until there were none left standing. And when it was all over, there lay three lifeless bodies surrounded by pools of blood-stained soil, forever bearing the scars of Tomoko's twisted rage.

Tomoko had done the unthinkable - she had sacrificed three of her closest friends to Kuchisake Onna, following through on her promise to leave Tomoko alone if she fulfilled this dark deed. And yet, despite being granted the promised beauty that she sought after, something still felt missing inside her heart. Her friends were gone and with them a piece of Tomoko's soul had been taken away as well. No amount of beauty could fill the void left behind by their deaths.

ΔΔΔ

Kappa

In the inner regions of Japan, there was a village nestled against the base of a mighty mountain. The village was a collection of straw and wooden houses, some with roofs of thatch, others with roofs of tin or steel. The buildings were spread out, separated by small farms and fields, separated by bamboo groves or rows of short pine trees.

You could smell the fish frying in the afternoon heat, smell smoke from a thousand cooking fires, smell the cattle and pigs and chickens, the scent of hay and dung and plant fertilizer. There was the smell of lingering rain from the day before.

The village was alive with the sounds of insects, dogs barking in the distance, the occasional sound of a chime or someone playing a flute. The streets seemed empty, but you could here people scurrying around, in and out of their houses. The sound of large wooden chopsticks striking a small gong in the town's shrine to the gods.

The streets were unpaved, and were littered with dirt and trash. The ceramic pots and bowls were old, chipped and worn, the well was a stone bowl, the fountain was made of ceramic.

The dry dirt of the road was cool on your bare feet, the muddy grass on either side was squishy, slick and cool, it hugged around your ankles. Insects buzzed harshly and grasshoppers leapt wildly, as if seeking to cast themselves up into the plains of a color they were no longer sure they could call green.

One day they dug through dirt, and the next day they dug through water, but it never made them happy at all. Sometimes it rained, and sometimes it didn't. Sometimes it was sunny, and sometimes it was not. Sometimes you grew up, and then sometimes you died. Sometimes you married, and then sometimes you didn't. Sometimes your teeth fell out, and then sometimes they were yanked out.

Sometimes you yelled, and sometimes you were yelled at. Sometimes you died, and sometimes you didn't. Sometimes you lived, and sometimes you breathed. Sometimes your heart was full, and sometimes it was empty. Sometimes you walked, and sometimes you ran. Sometimes they killed you, and sometimes they stuck you in a hole.

Sometimes you laughed, and sometimes you cried. Sometimes you were hungry, and sometimes you were full. Sometimes you felt good, and sometimes you felt bad. Sometimes you were happy, and sometimes you were sad.

All in All it was a normal village with normal people.

But nearby in a small pond lived a Kappa, a mischievous water spirit, which made this village not ordinary at all.

He was a miserable-looking creature, with a big head (which was sometimes mistaken for a pumpkin), a broad flat face, and a mouth which was almost always open. His eyes were large and round, and his nose was a little flat. His body was shaped like a papaya, and his long arms resembled that of a monkey's, but he had webbed fingers that enabled him to swim. His skin ranged in color from a dark green to a deep brown. He had large red eyes, and a mouth full of sharp teeth. The water-spirit seemed to be nothing more than a log. But as you approached, you saw a set of buckteeth jutting out of the water. His skin was slimy, like a eel or fish, and it was very cold, almost frozen.

Kappa was a master manipulator. He lured people into his waters by telling them he will play with them or that he had discovered a new treasure. When he pulled people into the water and dragged them to the bottom, he laughed and said "Gotcha!"

But in addition to his affinity for trickery, Kappa had a great fondness for cucumbers. He would often spend hours in the village's cucumber patch, munching on the crisp green vegetables until he was full. One day, as Kappa was feasting on his beloved cucumbers, he noticed that he was losing his powers. His once-strong arms and legs were growing weaker, and his magical abilities were fading away. At first, Kappa didn't understand what was happening. But then he realized that his love for cucumbers had caused him to neglect his duties as a water spirit. He had been spending all of his time eating cucumbers instead of causing mischief and playing pranks on the villagers.

With a heavy heart, Kappa realized that he would have to give up his beloved cucumbers in order to regain his powers. He knew that he had a responsibility to the villagers and to the river, and that he could not let his love for cucumbers get in the way of that. So Kappa made a difficult decision - he gave up his cucumbers and began to focus on his duties as a water spirit. He returned to the river and started playing pranks on the villagers once again, dragging them into the water and pulling them under.

At first, Kappa struggled without his cucumbers. He felt weak and powerless, and he missed the taste of his favorite vegetable. But as he continued to fulfill his duties, he began to regain his strength and his magical abilities. And as he played his pranks and caused mischief once again, Kappa knew that he had made the right decision. He may have lost his cucumbers, but he had regained his powers and his purpose as a water spirit. And that was all that mattered.

As Kappa resumed his pranks on the villagers, a young girl named Amaya was playing with her friends near the pond. Amaya, was a beautiful young girl. She was dainty, her cheeks were chubby. Her lips were a soft pink. She was wearing a dark, blue kimono, with a white obi. Around her waist was a colorful sash, with a matching blue fan tucked into the sash.

She crept closer to the edge of the pond, mesmerized by its stillness, her friends fading quickly from her consciousness. When she looked up, their voices were faint echoes in the distance and their figures had been swallowed up by the trees.

Unexpectedly, Kappa jumped in front of her.

Kappa: "Hey, little girl! What are you doing so close to my pond? Don't you know I like to play games with anyone who gets too close?"

Amaya: "I'm sorry, I didn't mean to intrude. I was just curious about the pond and wanted to get a better look."

Kappa: "Well, that's ok. But you don't seem scared, Don't you know me? I am Kappa, I like mischief and I like cucumbers. But I had to stay away from Cucumbers. They make me lazy and fat.

Amaya: I have heard about you, but you don't seem scary to me. I don't have a lot of friends. I have a few but they all talk about things that I am not interested in. Will you be my friend?

Kappa: Sure, Now how about we play a game? If you win, I'll give you one wish!"

Amaya: "Really? That sounds great! What kind of game do you want to play?"

Kappa: "We'll play a game of tag! I'll count to three and then try to catch you. If I don't catch you by the time I reach ten, then you win and can have your wish!"

Amaya: Sure, be informed that I am faster than a hare.

Kappa: I am faster than you, One,Two,Three...

Amaya was quick but the wet mud near the pond made her slip. Kappa ran and grabbed her quickly. Kappa's hand was like an iron grip around her wrist, and the joy in his eyes was replaced with one of malicious intent. With a demented grin on his face, he dragged her towards the water, knowing full well what he planned to do - scare her senseless. Her screams were music to his ears as he held her down under the surface, convinced it was all just a harmless game.

At first, she sputtered and thrashed about beneath him, but soon her movements became weaker and weaker. It wasn't until he noticed the abject terror in her eyes that Kappa realized he had gone too far. Cold dread trickled through him, spreading like ice in his veins. The girl's body went limp beneath him, and panic surged through Kappa as he freed her from his grasp. He dragged her back to shallow waters where she lay motionless. Kappa tried to revive her but it was too late. Kappa watched in horror, knowing that this would haunt him for the rest of his life.

When the villagers discovered Kappa's crime, they were livid. They had been suspicious of his intentions for a while, but now they wanted retribution. Fury sparked within them as they formed an angry mob and hunted him down, their cries of vengeance ringing through the air. Desperate to escape their wrath, Kappa pleaded for mercy, professing his innocence and begging for forgiveness. But his pleas fell on deaf ears, and he was pelted with stones and sticks until he plunged into the river in terror.

Kappa shuddered in fear as he swam through the river, desperately trying to keep himself hidden. He was sure that the villagers were still after him and had no idea how he could possibly make up for what he had done. But as he rounded a bend one night, he came upon a circle of river spirits wailing and mourning the death of their own kind. A young spirit had been playing recklessly with humans and paid the ultimate price - it hit Kappa like a bolt of lightning - he wasn't alone in his mischievous ways; his pranks had caused harm too.

He saw the pain and sorrow in the eyes of the other spirits, and he knew that he needed to do something to make amends.

He vowed to never harm humans again, and to make sure that other spirits remembered the lesson he had learned. He spoke to the other spirits of how his selfishness had led to tragedy - and together they agreed not to meddle in human affairs anymore.

He began to share with them stories of his misadventures, hoping they would find some solace in his tales. As he spoke, the spirits gradually started to laugh, and soon their laughter echoed through the entire river.

Kappa realized then that there was still hope for him - if he could make even one person laugh or smile each day, then maybe he could one day be forgiven by both the humans and the other spirits. With a newfound sense of purpose, Kappa vowed to continue making mischief while also doing good deeds whenever possible.

With their help, Kappa went back to the village and offered to help in any way he could. He spent his days working in the fields, helping the villagers tend to their crops and animals. And at night, he used his magical abilities to protect the village from danger. Slowly but surely, the villagers began to forgive Kappa for what he had done. They saw the changes in him, and they realized that he was truly sorry for his actions.

And in time, Kappa became an important and respected member of the community. He never forgot the little girl who had lost her life because of his actions. But he knew that he had learned a valuable lesson about the power of his mischief, and he vowed to use it for good instead of harm.

ΔΔΔ

Jengu

The depths of the African sea are a vast and mysterious expanse filled with exotic creatures. The deep blue waters ripple and glow with an iridescent light, and the shadows of larger fish dart around in the darkness. Schools of colorful fish glide through the depths, and vast coral reefs form intricate webs of life. There are strange and wondrous treasures to be found in the darkness, and the depths of the sea remain a constant source of fascination.

They have a musky, earthy scent. It's salty and briny with a hint of sea life pungency, mixed with the subtle smells of seaweed and algae. A whiff of something ancient, like a forgotten treasure waiting to be discovered. A raw and wet cure, an infinite abyss of blue sky and salt.

Among these wonders, lived a beautiful and powerful Jengu, a mermaid-like creature, who ruled the waters near Mount Fako with her mesmerizing voice and enchanting beauty. Jengu was an exquisite creature, her skin glistening like a pearl in the moonlight of the deep sea. Her body was slender and graceful, with a shining tail and fins of the deepest blue. Her long hair cascaded down her back like a midnight waterfall, and her eyes sparkled with wisdom and knowledge. She carried herself with an aura of strength and power that radiated through the waters around her. She sang with a voice like a beautiful symphony, captivating all who hear it.

Jengu had a tantalizing scent that was both sweet and salty, like a heady mix of fresh sea air and exotic spices. Her skin scented with the aroma of honeysuckle, jasmine, and orange blossoms, and her hair had a delicate yet alluring fragrance that can't be resisted. There was a hint of mystery in her wake, a subtle yet unmistakable smell of something magical and ancient.

One day, while she was exploring the sea, she met a handsome man named Lekan. Lekan was a tall and broad-shouldered figure with clear, bright blue eyes and tanned skin. His hair was black, cut short and tight to his head, giving him a noble and regal air. He moved through the water with a strong, confident grace that was mesmerizing to watch. His skin was smooth and warm to the touch, and he had an air of power around him that could be felt by anyone in his presence. He moved gracefully through the water like a graceful dolphin, and his muscles were strong and powerful like a true sea prince.

They both fell madly and deeply in love. Starting with a teenage like attraction where they couldnt take their hands of each other, but slowly maturing into a love for the ages. Jengu and Lekan's love seemed to know no bounds, their days filled with exploration of the furious sea and stories that encircled them like an enchanted fog. As their bond strengthened, two children were born into the family, who shared the same captivating voice and stunning beauty as their mother, bewitching everyone who encountered them.

However, as time passed, Jengu began to change. She became restless and dissatisfied with her life underwater. The more she explored the depths of the sea, the more she craved for the taste of human flesh.

Jengu: "Lekan, my love, do you ever get tired of the sea? Of always living underwater?"

Lekan: "No, my dear. This is where we belong. Our home is in the water, and we are happiest here."

Jengu: "But I feel restless, Lekan. I want something more. Something different."

Lekan: "What do you mean, Jengu?"

Jengu: "I don't know, Lekan. I just feel like there's something missing. Something I need to explore."

Lekan: "Be careful, Jengu. The ocean is vast, and there are dangers that even we cannot imagine."

Jengu: "I'll be careful, Lekan. I promise."

Every night, she would leave their home in the seafloor and go on a rampage, devouring any sailor that crossed her path. Lekan was heartsick, desperately trying to find a way to save his beloved from her monstrous appetite.

He was devastated by Jengu's transformation and begged her to stop, but she refused to listen.

Lekan: "Jengu, what have you done? This is not who you are!"

Jengu: "I can't help it, Lekan. The taste of their flesh and blood is too tempting. I must have more."

Lekan: "You're endangering yourself and our children, Jengu. You must stop before it's too late."

Jengu: "I can't stop, Lekan. I won't stop."

Lekan: "You have to stop Jengu, for our love, for our children."

But Jengu continued on her wretched path, her lust for all things - flesh and blood took her on a ravaging course that consumed her day by day.

One night, as Lekan searched for Jengu, he stumbled upon a mysterious man sitting on a rock at the edge of the sea. The man was tall and thin, with a regal air about him. His skin was weathered and dark, and his eyes were bright and piercing. His hair was long and grey, and he was wearing a deep blue robe that sweeps the ground. He sat on a large rock at the edge of the sea, looking out into the distance with a peaceful expression on his face.

He was shaped like a dark brown oval, but with black arms and legs that were like torn canvas flapping in the wind. He had a huge starfish hand and there was a thin shard of ebony covering his mouth. He had a boat that descended from a red storm cloud. The boat was like a long underground river, with a huge gaping mouth in the front and a kingfisher eye that burned red when it flared.

His eyes looked full of knowledge and wisdom beyond what Lekan could comprehend. He uttered a dire warning to Lekan that if he didn't acquire the Amulet of Oya before sunrise and tie it around her neck, her hunger would be forever unquenchable. He revealed that the only thing that could end her monstrous appetite was an ancient charm located on a forsaken island in the deep sea, guarded by the elderly and powerful sea goddess Yemaya. If Lekan failed to find it in time, Jengu would remain a ravenous monster for eternity.

Without hesitation, Lekan set out on his quest to find this mysterious amulet and save his beloved Jengu from her fate. After days of searching and struggling against monsters of the deep sea, he finally reached Yemaya's island. The sight that greeted him was breathtaking; huge mountains of crystal blue and turquoise, filled with bright coral reefs where exotic creatures swam and played. The air was filled with the sweet smell of flowers, their petals dancing in the breeze. He could feel a powerful energy radiating from the island, a deep sense of peace that filled his soul with hope and courage.

Despite his fear, Lekan bravely ventured further into the island in search for the amulet. Suddenly, he found himself face to face with a giant creature with eyes like burning coals and claws as sharp as daggers. It roared at him like thunder, challenging him to battle for the sacred relic he sought.

Lekan held his ground bravely and fought back fiercely despite being outnumbered by enemies tenfold. He swung his fists wildly like thunderbolts and his feet kicked at them like lightning. Finally, he was able to vanquish them showing his true prowess and why he was called the Prince of Thunder.

Lekan was finally face to face with the Sea Goddess. She was a majestic figure that radiated an ethereal beauty. Her long, flowing hair like a cascading waterfall of white foam and her skin glistened like the sea on a moonless night. Her eyes were a deep blue that reflected the depths of the ocean, and her lips were full and pink like a rosebud. Her garments floated around her like seaweed, and she carried a staff inlaid with glowing pearl and adorned with a shimmering crescent moon.

The sea goddess carried the smell of sweet jasmine mixed with the salty ocean air, like a hint of paradise far away from the travails of everyday life. A whiff of fresh ocean spray lingered around her, bringing with it the promise of new adventure. Her presence was large and her eyes were radiant and clear, filled with an old wonder that captivated Lekan and left him awestruck.

The sea goddess welcomed him with open arms and presented him with The Amulet of Oya – a glowing necklace made of starlight and moonlight which had the power to control Jengu's beastly urges.

Armed with this powerful gift from Yemaya, Lekan raced back to their underwater castle in time for sunrise. Lekan called out to her, "Jengu, How are you? How are our children? I long to see them. Come out, my love." Lekan didn't get any response. He kept knocking at the door but Lekan didn't hear anything. Finally out of frustration, Lekan burst open the door.

Jengu was there, but Lekan didn't recognize her anymore. Her eyes were once so full of life and love, but now they were empty and soulless. As he looked around he saw the lifeless, headless corpses of their children - his children, her children. He couldn't understand how she could have done this, killed the ones that once meant more to her than anything else. Tears streamed down his face as he uttered "How could you do this to our own children?" Jengu's response included a slurping noise coming from inside her blood-soaked mouth. It was too much for Lekan; he lunged at her, taking her neck in his hands and choking her with anger and pain radiating through him. Jengu struggled against him trying desperately to free herself, but he was far too strong. When she finally died, a piece of their child's eye fell out of her mouth.

Lekan was now standing alone on the beach, his head bowed low as the waves of the sea crashed against the shore. He stared out into the horizon, his eyes distant and without hope. The moonlight reflected on his skin, and the soft breeze blew against his face. He took his first steps into the sea, the water surrounding him like a cocoon, taking away all the pain and suffering he experienced at Jengu's hands. He submerged himself, and with each passing moment, was further taken away from the memory of Jengu, until he eventually disappeared into the depths of the sea.

ΔΔΔ

Selkie

Ancient Scotland was characterized by lush rolling hills of green, vast stretches of heather-covered moors, and rugged mountains rising sharply above the horizon. The misty lochs and glens were filled with ancient forests, while the lochs and bays of the North Sea were speckled with small islands. It had a fresh, earthy smell; the smell of wildflowers, heather and gorse after a rainfall; the salty sea air tinged with a hint of peaty smoke from nearby bonfires; and the smell of new-mown grass after a summer shower.

There was a forest, which was green and alive, and a castle that spiraled up a hill, and children playing on the shore, and birds in nests, and a cool breeze, and a single star in a purple sky.

Beyond those forests, lay the North Sea. The North Sea was a deep, unending sapphire blue, that stretched out to the horizon as far as the eye could see. Its surface was cool and inviting, sparkling with the reflection of the stars and moon, beckoning you with its depths. The air was filled with the smell of salt and sea, and an air of mystery that lingered in its bowels. Small white-capped waves lapped against the shore, creating an ebb and flow that was both soothing and dangerous. It smelled like salty air, fresh seaweed and fish, moss and fragrant flowers. It was a mixture of the ocean's calm and wildness, its warmth and its chill.

The sea was once filled with flora and fauna so wonderful and breath taking that they no longer felt real now. One of them was a large, yellow rectangle spinning on its side, like a giant sunflower. The colors were unfamiliar but evocative, and the shape was mesmerizing—everything was so simple, yet so striking. The other one—well, it was very yellow, and shiny. There was a single star at its center. It was indescribable - maybe deep blue or blue-green, and the land below was dotted with tiny squares in the colors of oranges and reds and purples, which could have been flowers, or maybe jewels? Despite all of this brightness, everything seemed to be calling out to people from far, far away. The bright light, the sparkles of yellow, the warmth and sparkles of orange and red and purple. It felt like falling into a gigantic painting, falling and falling, until, again, everything faded to black.

In those once magical blue waters of the North Sea of Scotland, there lived a community of seal-folk known as the Selkies. Selkies were humanoids with seal-like features. They had short, thick fur covering their bodies, though the color and pattern were particular to each individual. Many of the Selkies had a softer, smoother fur on their chests, and their manes of hair also came in a variety of colors. They had a slight smell of the sea, not too strong, but fresh and clean. They had a human-like intelligence, but tended to be playful and mischievous, like dolphins.

Selkies were capable of vocalizing in a variety of ways, including human speech, high-pitched chirps, and low-pitched growls. Their language was one of the few animal languages that was similar to that of humans. They were very fun-loving and playful, so they were usually singing songs, telling jokes, and making up funny noises. But they would gladly bite off a limb of anyone if they sensed danger.

They were once said to be close to humans but in what way no one could describe. They loved all kinds of human things, like hugs, candy, and stories. Beautiful and graceful, they were said to move to the plaintive strains of music. They often grouped together, down the profundity of the sea and across the shores, along the reeds and sea weeds, sitting and standing in clusters, sometimes wrapped in dark robes, whispering and occasionally howling, with their hands stretched back toward the shadows they had come from.

They were known for their beauty, their gentle nature, and their magical ability to transform into humans by shedding their seal skins. In human form, they were the most enchanting creatures, with their long flowing hair, sparkling eyes, and ethereal voices.

The Selkies, however, lived in fear of humans now, who were known to hunt them for their valuable skins. One such Selkie, named Selena, had a deep fascination with the human world. Selena with her healthy, rosy cheeks, her vibrant, shiny hair and deep, dark eyes. Her dark skin was warm to the touch and smooth. Her smile was warm and comforting. Her footsteps were quiet, like a mountain cat. She was slender, but not frail or weak. Her voice was kind and loving. It was as sweet as honey and as soothing as a mother's lullaby. She spoke in a whisper, like gentle summer rain.

She would spend hours watching the humans from the safety of the sea, wondering what it would be like to walk on land, to feel the sun on her skin, and to breathe the air that humans breathed. She wanted to feel the sand beneath her feet, the warmth of the sun on her face, the sound of the waves rolling in, the taste of the salt water in her mouth, the smell of the ocean and the feeling of the wind from the sea.

One day, while she was exploring the coast, she saw a young fisherman named Liam wash up to the shores, unconscious and injured in a storm. She would often see Liam with his group of fisherman going deep in into the North Sea and coming back with nets full of fish for their families. Selena noticed that he was young, but older than her. He had a nice face, a warm smile. His voice was sweet, like honey. He had brown, curly hair, and bright green eyes. His skin was pale, but not sickly pale. His body was strong and muscular, but not bulky. His hands were big, but not scary big. His shoulders were broad, but not frighteningly so. His voice was deep as well, but it held a melody, like a song. Selena had often wondered what it would be like to talk to a human like him, touch him, caress him.

Without hesitation, Selena transformed into her human form,

wrapped Liam in her seal skin, and carried him to safety. His clothes were worn, but comfortable. He had callouses from years at sea, like scales, across his palms and the pads of his fingers. He had a scar on his right hand, from when he was a boy, when his father taught him how to gut and clean a fish. He had a scar on his left arm, from when a great white bit him, just below his elbow. He had a chiseled jaw and piercing eyes, magnetic and dark, save for two thin dead rivers that scrolled through them like paint, not unlike a blind man's eyes; all blackness, with a white pinprick in them.

Liam and Selena were instantly drawn to one another, spending more and more time together as he recovered from his injuries. They would walk along the beach and talk for hours, their deep connection forming a bond that was impossible to break. As much as Selena wanted to be with Liam, she was terrified of what might happen if he ever discovered her secret—that she was a selkie who could transform back into her true form only if she kept her magical seal skin safe. She knew that if Liam ever found out about it, he might take her seal skin away from her and trap her in human form forever.

One day, while Liam was out fishing, Selena went for a swim and left her seal skin on the beach. When Selena returned from her swim, she knew something was wrong. She could sense it in the air. She searched frantically for her seal skin, but it was nowhere to be found. Her heart sank as she knew what Liam had done. She turned to him, anger and hurt etched across her face.

"Why would you do this, Liam?" she demanded, her voice trembling with emotion.

"I couldn't bear the thought of losing you," Liam replied, his own voice laced with sadness. "I know I should have never taken your skin, but I couldn't help myself. I want to spend the rest of my life with you, Selena."

Selena's eyes softened slightly as she realized the depth of Liam's love for her. But she also knew that without her seal skin, she would be trapped on land forever. She took a deep breath and spoke, "Liam, you have to give my seal skin back. I can't stay on land forever, I'll die without it."

Liam's eyes widened in shock as he heard the desperation in her voice. "I had no idea," he muttered, his voice quiet. "I'm so sorry, Selena. I'll give your skin back to you, I promise."

Selena nodded, her heart aching with love and sacrifice. She knew that giving up her life on land with Liam was the right thing to do. She could never fully be herself without her seal skin, and Liam deserved to live his life with someone who could love him in the way he deserved.

But before she could return to the sea, Liam offered to come with her. He was willing to give up his life on land and be with her in the sea, bound together by their love. Selena was overwhelmed by his offer and even more so by the depth of his love for her. She accepted without hesitation, knowing that this was a chance for them to be together forever.

So the two of them returned to the beach and Liam found her seal skin where he had hidden it beneath a pile of pebbles. He presented it to Selena who smiled lovingly as she held it in her hands. With a deep breath, Selena transformed back into her true form and beckoned Liam into the water with her so they could continue their journey together—hand in hand—beneath the waves.

Once they entered the ocean, Selena and Liam were met with a world of breathtaking beauty. Everywhere they looked there were vibrant coral reefs and colorful schools of fish darting around them. The air was filled with the sound of dolphins singing and whales breaching the surface, sending sprays of sea foam in all directions. They dove deeper beneath the waves, exploring the depths of the ocean and discovering its many wonders. As they traveled deeper into this unknown world, Selena and Liam encountered creatures such as octopuses, seahorses, starfish, eels, jellyfish, stingrays and more. They marveled at each new discovery as if it were their first time seeing these creatures up close.

Selena showed Liam her secret hideaway—a hidden cove surrounded by rock walls that sheltered them from the rest of the sea. Here they could rest peacefully amongst an array of tropical reef fish who seemed to recognize Selena's presence in their midst. It was here that Selena would tell stories about her life on land before she became a selkie—stories about family reunions around bonfires on summer nights or about running through meadows at sunset with her friends when she was younger.

After a few weeks of exploring, Liam and Selena returned to the surface for air. They looked around in awe as they realized how far their love had taken them. Eventually, Liam knew it was time to go back to land and bid goodbye to his family and friends.

But Liam was no ordinary family man. He was a notorious selkie poacher, who used every resource to track down the creatures. Liam had a hardened expression, and lack of empathy for anything that crossed his path. His Love Story with Selena was not organic—it was part of Liam's grand scheme to make money by harvesting selkies for their valuable treasures.

Liam's eagerness to capture and enslave all of the selkies was evident as he returned to the beach with his hunting posse. He had a cruel glint in his eye as he surveyed the shore, looking for any sign of Selena. His heart raced with a ferocious hunger for the selkies and he was determined to hunt once and for all these mysterious creatures and destroy their settlements.

The hunt soon began as Liam's men combed through the depths of the sea, searching every nook and cranny for evidence of a selkie's presence. They scattered across the water like locusts, leaving destruction in their wake as they searched relentlessly. But wherever they went, Selena remained hidden; her secret hiding place safe from their probing eyes. But Liam knew exactly where she was.

It wasn't long before their search led them straight to her secret cove beneath the waves. With swift precision, they filled the water with nets and harpoons before storming into her refuge with darkness in their hearts. In an instant, death surround Selena as she watched helplessly while Liam and his gang slaughtered every single selkie in sight—no matter if they were young or old—leaving behind only a tide of blood that stained the sea floor red.

No mercy was shown as Liam ruthlessly captured those who remained alive before dragging them back onto shore where they would be sold off like commodities to buyers from around the world who desired these enigmatic creatures for their own selfish gain. Selena could only stand in horror as she watched her people be taken away one by one until there were none left alive.

As Liam stood victorious on the beach after his mass slaughter of selkies, Selena emerged from beneath the waves in a final act of desperation to save her people from extinction. She begged him to spare their lives if only out of respect for what they shared together during their brief time together in this universe.

Selena stared helplessly at Liam as he approached until he stood right in front of her, an icy smirk playing on his lips as he drew near enough for Selena to smell his fishy breath against her face as he spoke: "This is what you get for thinking you can escape me." With those final words uttered between them, Liam raised up his spear and drove it deep into Selena's chest with one powerful thrust. Blood spilled out from the wound and pooled around both of them in a crimson tide, washing away any remaining hope for freedom that might have still lingered within Selena's heart until finally - mercifully - she takes one last gasp of air before slipping away.

ΔΔΔ

Baba Yaga

A remote forest in Russia, unknown and untouchable to the human kind was shrouded in fog and mystery, with snow-dusted evergreens reaching high into the sky. The snowdrifts were pristine, untouched by human hands and the sun cast an eerie blue light through the canopy of trees. As you walked through this enchanted forest, you could hear the whisper of the wind rustling through the branches. You might even catch a glimpse of a fox or a hare darting away through the snow.

It was a vast land with tall trees and winding pathways. The trees were dark and twisted, their branches entwined with each other. The air was brisk and the sky was filled with grey clouds. The forest floor was slithering with creatures, magnificent and dangerous, making it seem as if it's a forbidden place that's full of secrets and danger.

A dilapidated old cabin of dark wood and iron stood on a grassy knoll in a forest of old-growth trees with silver trunks, so tall and stately that their tops vanished into the mist. The cabin seemed out of place, for it had been weathered by storms and beaten by seasons, its pockmarked planks and crooked porch railings giving it the appearance of a dour old man whose face was studied in a thousand wrinkles. The roof, once steep and proud, was now sagging and sloping, having lost the battle with the elements. In some places, the shingles were all but gone, leaving only the bare, warped boards to protect the cabin from the rain spattering through the air. Moss grew like a fungus on the walls of the cabin, and it was furnished with only a few pieces of furniture, such as a narrow, flat bed and wooden chair.

Inside the infamous Baba Yaga, the ogress of all ogres hunched against the wall. Her nose was long and crooked, her hair was unkempt and her mouth was full of yellowed, rotten teeth. Her clothes were a dirty and raggedy, patched with the skins of animals and the hides of children. She was a tall and thin woman who looked very wrinkly, with an old and worn face that's full of cracks, like a dried riverbed. Her nose looked like a finger, with one eye missing and one tooth blackened, like an old tree's branch that's been broken and burned by lightning.

Her breath smelled of decaying flesh, the products of her meals were still inside of her, decaying. Her skin smelled like the forest after a rain, not a fresh rain, but a rain that had soaked the trees and made their skin slick and stinky, with a hint that something is rotting. Her clothes smelled like the forest floor, full of rotting fungi, poison and mold. Legends said her flesh would taste of death and decay, like meat left out in the sun to rot. Her blood would taste of the earth, and iron, which she had been soaking in for a long time.

Baba Yaga was a fleet of ogres in a fleet of cars flying tandem to a fleet of speeding black-eyed rainclouds: a fleet of teeth and claws and scales sunning themselves on wide white macadam roads that led in every direction, and inevitably leading home. She was a fleet of eyes charting silver-soared sunrises, and all the stars tumbling down to earth, and the moons with their loci of cities. She was a fleet of spiders building webs in the crook-black night, and a fleet of lions wading in the red water. She was a fleet of flowers blooming, and a fleet of bees dancing between them, and the noise of their dancing the sound of a green, green forest teeming with life and death. She was a fleet of coats and spoons, and a fleet of needles, and all of these things stitched together, and a fleet of stories that have yet to be told.

Baba Yaga was tired. Her bones creaked, her skin sagged, and the time she had seen pass by seemed to forever haunt her. The earth had been destroyed countless times in her years, each time ending in more death and suffering than before. She had seen world wars take place and leave behind a wasteland of corpses and ash. But now there was nothing left that she hadn't already experienced and the ancient ogress only craved a single thing: rest. Each night Baba Yaga would sink into her armchair and sip at her bowl of children soup, watching the flames dance in the hearth as she counted away yet another day of quiet and seclusion.

But as much as she cherished these respites from the tumult of life, even Baba Yaga's stony heart still yearned for adventure every now and again. And so each night, before she drifted off to sleep, the old woman would recall stories from days past to no one in particular - tales of brave heroes, ambitious despots, and lovers reunited against all odds – allowing herself a momentary glimpse into a wilder world than her own.

Still, Baba Yaga held onto hope that one day it would all be over and she'd have that moment of reprieve she so desperately desired. That maybe one day she could sleep without always looking over her shoulder; without hearing the screams from her memories ringing in her ears; without feeling the regret that came with every decision she made over centuries of existence. She yearned for that day—that moment—to come and give her the peace at last.

The morning sun cast an eerie light on the house of Baba Yaga, like a sallow beacon of death. A gnarled, withered hand reached out from behind her door and pulled in a sheet of parchment paper that had been slipped underneath. She unfurled it slowly, bracing herself for what was to come. Its crisp lettering branded itself into her eyes: "I'm coming for you, Baba Yaga. You cannot hide from me." Her heart sunk into her stomach; she knew this wasn't some idle threat... it was the Boogeyman.

The Boogeyman was a creature like no other, one of the few in existence who could truly cause harm to the immortal Baba Yaga. He was said to be a being of pure chaos, laughing maniacally as he spread fear across the lands. Some said he had horns and hooves like a beast, pointing sharp claws that struck terror into anyone who looked upon them. Others said his eyes glowed with an iridescent yellow-green that caused their souls to freeze in their tracks with fear. And everyone agreed that his sinister smile revealed two rows of razor-sharp teeth that made even grown men cower in dread.

Baba Yaga's hands trembled as she held the parchment tight against her chest. The Boogeyman was coming for her, and there was nowhere she could run.

Baba Yaga started hunting more, aware that she had to be stronger now to face the dreaded Boogeyman. She commanded her flock of black geese to circle the skies looking for children. Children she could turn into soup and bones and get stronger for the days to come. But days turned into weeks and months, but there was no sign of the Boogeyman. Until one day.

With a thunderous crack, the door to Baba Yaga's cottage opened. The figure was cloaked in darkness, from its flaming red eyes to its razor sharp claws. This was the Boogeyman, an unstoppable creature of nightmares, who roamed the lands with no care for life or mercy. Baba Yaga stared into its burning gaze and felt a chill take hold of her body.

The Boogeyman took a step forward and spoke in a solemn voice - 'You thought you could outwit me? You were wrong. I know your every move, your every thought. I can be anywhere at any time, and no force on Earth can stop me. I'm going to make you pay for Olga, Sergei and all the children you've eaten and all the lives you've ruined."

Baba Yaga's veins surged with dread as her mind comprehended the truth of the Boogeyman's words. She was trapped in a corner with no hope of flight or victory. The Boogeyman rushed towards her, his face twisted with anger. He grabbed hold of Baba Yaga and threw her to the ground with a violent thud. Baba Yaga attempted to fight back, but her efforts were futile against the monster's power. The Boogeyman sneered at her, exposing his razor-sharp teeth. "After all these years, I've finally found you Baba Yaga," he snarled. "Now it's time for you to pay for every life you've destroyed and every child you've devoured."

Baba Yaga accepted her fate as she realized there was no escape from this terror. But then, something strange happened - an insane laughter erupted from deep within Baba Yaga's chest. It filled the forest with its wild cackles and eerie chuckles. With each syllable, Baba Yaga felt her strength returning.

"What's so funny?" the Boogeyman demanded. "You think you can defeat me?" Baba Yaga said, still chuckling. "You're nothing compared to the horrors I've faced. You're nothing compared to the darkness that resides within me." And with that, Baba Yaga transformed into a monstrous creature. Her eyes turned blood-red, and her skin stretched and twisted until it was covered in spikes. The Boogeyman was caught off guard, and Baba Yaga took the opportunity to strike.

The Boogeyman and Baba Yaga locked in combat, their faces twisted with rage as they tore flesh from bone. The two were locked in a deadly embrace, the Boogeyman's talons trying to pierce Baba Yaga's eyes, her claws digging into the Boogeyman's throat. The blood splattered across the ground like a child's finger painting, wild and untamed, but with a grotesque beauty. Each drop a violent explosion, a beautiful explosion of red.

The Boogeyman's feet kicked at the dark, wet soil, leaving a small crater in its wake. Baba Yaga's hands were covered in blood and fur and mud as she clawed at the Boogeyman's chest. The Boogeyman raked back, across Baba Yaga's skin, opening deep cuts that bled freely, the blood ed onto the forest floor. Baba Yaga's claws again ripped into the Boogeyman's flesh, pinning him to the ground, the blood trickled down his body and pools upon the ground. Each drop a rivulet of life.

They fought with all their strength and wickedness, slashing a path to the other somewhat dead and somewhat not. These were perversions of the human form, each capable of geometrically increasing the other's agony. Mouths opened; they bit. They tore and they rent, but in the end, the tearing seemed unending. They were hungrily tearing away at each other, their bodies succumbing to the time of the hunter. They were equal in their unhandsomeness.

But, Baba Yaga's transformation gave her a strength that was unmatched, and she finally managed to pin the Boogeyman down. Baba Yaga's facial features twisted with rage as she threw the Boogeyman to the ground. Orange fire danced behind her as if mocking the Boogeyman's futile act of vengeance. Baba Yaga's face was ferocious, her eyes burning red with a deep, primal rage.

Baba Yaga began to chant an ancient spell, her voice a deep and powerful rumble. The words echoed in the silent forest, bouncing off the trees as if they were alive. Baba Yaga's chanting grew louder and more intense as she called upon the darkness of the woods for power. The Boogeyman screamed in agony as the darkness descended upon him, consuming his body with its unceasing hunger. His screams were silenced as he was slowly obliterated by the force of Baba Yaga's spell, until all that remained was a pile of ashes and bones.

Baba Yaga surveyed the aftermath, her breath tight in her chest. Tears pricked her eyes and a chill passed through her body as the reality of what she had done settled over her. The Boogeyman was gone, and yet...she felt so hollow inside. She had used the darkest aspects of herself to win that day, and no matter how hard she tried, Baba Yaga could not ignore it completely.

Her decision was made; from then on, she'd live out her life further deep in the forest, far away from any semblance of civilization. Maybe if she stayed here long enough, the fear and loathing would fade away into oblivion. But deep down she knew that it wouldn't be so easy. The darkness inside her would never truly go away—it would always remain a part of who she was. Baba Yaga sank to the ground, realizing that the fight against herself had only just begun.

$$\Delta\Delta\Delta$$

Babi Ngepet

Adit and Nagbad had an air of determination and a look of hopelessness in their faces. They were both wearing worn out clothing, but their hands were tightly clasped, showing their unwavering bond. Adit had short dark hair, while Nagbad's was cropped short and lighter in color. They both sat on the sand, looking out at the sea in front of them with a mix of fear and determination.

They had been here many times before, but this time was different. They had lost it all. It was gone. The money they'd so thoughtfully acquired from their last job, now vanished in a single night. Lost to the world of endless gambling. But it wasn't just their own money that was gone - far worse, they had amassed huge debts as well.

Their mistakes weighed heavy on them like an anvil chained to an ankle, dragging them further and further into despair. They had come with hope, with dreams of making more than what they had, only to find themselves spiraling ever downward into the abyss of debt and consequence.

In the darkness of defeat, they contemplated the saying: "the house always wins". Yet still, they could not help but be drawn back to the tables, offering up another chance at salvation even if it meant risking yet more ruin.

The thrill of playing seemed to take over their being, like a drug that promised pleasure yet only brought sorrow in its wake. Still, the urge to prove themselves greater than the odds kept them returning again and again; until soon all of those who were once close companions were gone - replaced by hollow faces casting long shadows across green felt tables, where luck and life's fortunes could both be won or lost within a few short moments.

For these gamblers, there was no escape from addiction; no way out of having put too much faith in luck when wisdom so desperately should have been heeded instead.

"Are you sure about this, Adit?" Nagbad asked, his voice quivering as he clutched Adit's hand tighter.

Adit's mind raced with possibilities of what could happen if they succeeded. "Yes," he said firmly, trying to mask the fear in his voice. "The legend says those who embrace Babi Ngepet can have anything they want...but at a price."

Babi Ngepet was the legendary Boar Demon. Though there were various stories about how Babi Ngepet looked, there was one which became real with the incessant recounts. It was supposed to be a black figure shrouded in a long, dark cloak with a pointed hood that obscured its face. Its hands were thin and bony, and it moved slowly, slithering around with a hiss. Its eyes glowed a sickly yellow and its mouth was filled with sharp fangs. Its presence brought an eerie chill to the air, and its cold aura of power could be felt by all in its presence.

Nagbad nodded, and the pair looked out into the sea, the waves lapping their feet. "What ingredients do we need?" he asked. Adit thought for a moment. "We need cempoalxochitl flowers, dragon's blood, and a jar of black honey." He paused for a beat, then added: "And a black chicken."

Nagbad shuddered at the thought of the black chicken, but he steeled himself and stood up. "Let's go," he said, leading the way.

The sun was setting as the two ventured into the forest. With each step, their hope was growing; the legend had become a reality. It seemed almost too good to be true.

They searched the shadows for the ingredients they needed. The cempoalxochitl flowers were easy to find; they glowed in the darkness like stars. After a few hours of searching, they finally found the dragon's blood and black honey. But the black chicken proved more elusive.

Finally, after hours of searching, they stumbled upon a small hut in the woods. Inside, they found a black chicken, standing in the corner, watching them with its beady eyes.

Adit and Nagbad looked at each other, their faces tense with anticipation. They had found everything they needed. It was time to put their plan into action.

The two made their way back to the beach, their footsteps heavy with anticipation. When they arrived, they built a small fire and started to prepare the ingredients. Adit crushed the cempoalxochitl flowers and added them to the concoction, as well as the dragon's blood and black honey. He stirred the mixture and chanted the ancient words of Babi Ngepet.

The chicken squawked wildly as Adit grabbed it and laid it in the middle of the circle they had drawn in the sand. He slit its throat and let its blood mix with the other ingredients.

His chant grew louder and louder until the circle erupted with a loud explosion. Adit and Nagbad were thrown back by the force of the blast, and when they opened their eyes, they saw a figure standing before them.

Babi Ngepet, had come to life.

Adit and Nagbad watched in awe as the figure rose from the ground and floated above them. It was an ancient being, its face distorted with rage and its body shrouded in a dark cloak. It looked at them with eyes full of hatred, and Adit could not help but tremble in fear.

The figure spoke in a voice that sounded like the thunder of a storm. "You have summoned me, selfish mortals. You will get all the riches in the world, but you must also pay a price. Are you ready to pay the price?" It's voice echoed through the night.

Adit and Nagbad looked at each other in terror, they knew they had come too far to go back now. Adit fetched all his might and trembled to Babi Ngpet, "We are ready to pay the price."

A furious screech filled the air, and Babi Ngepet suddenly transformed before their eyes. Its coarse fur turned to shimmering skin, but the tusks remained the same. "One of you will tragically succumb to my form," it cackled wickedly, its words ringing in their ears like an eerie warning from beyond death. "The demon boar can then meander through the village, scratching against walls and furniture as money, gold, and jewelry will disappear mysteriously into its black robes. One of you will stay here with a candle that must be flickered on top of a basin of water. If the flame dimms or shakes, it's a sign of danger for you, meaning you have been caught in the act or are turning back into your human form. Once you are satisfied with your loot, come back here. Don't try to run away from me. I am Babi Ngepet, the Demon Boar, I will haunt you for the rest of your lives."

Adit was struck with terror, but he knew what he had to do. He took a deep breath and nodded to Babi Ngepet. He then closed his eyes, and when he opened them again, he felt a strange power coursing through him. His body changed into a giant boar with sharp tusks and coarse fur that glowed in the darkness. He was the demon boar now, ready to wreak havoc upon the village.

He charged out of their camp, crashing through walls and furniture as people screamed in fear and ran away from him. Adit's rampage continued for hours on end as he stole money, gold, jewelry and other precious items from unsuspecting villagers. In his fury he even killed some of them who tried to stand up against him or deny him his prize.

Adit felt the weight of guilt pressing down upon him as he finally returned to camp, where Babi Ngepet was waiting for him. It had a sinister smile on its face as it spoke, telling Adit that he had done well. The words faded away like a fog in the night air and Adit looked around at all the treasures that were now his – riches taken from the village that wasn't his own.

He slowly turned towards Nagbad, with sadness washing over him like a wave. In the corner of his eye he saw Babi Ngepet looming closer to his partner-in-crime and Adit wanted nothing more than to intervene and save Nagbad's life. But instead, he stood helplessly by, silently pleading with fate to turn its course while knowing deep down it would not listen.

Nagbad didn't stand a chance against Babi Ngepet's power and Adit watched in horror as his friend crumpled to the ground beneath the beast's might. He closed his eyes and squeezed them tight so tightly that tears began to flow, yet he couldn't bring himself to look away from the scene unfolding before him - a scene in which he was directly responsible for.

The price for their plunder that night seemed too great for either of them to bear; Nagbad had paid the ultimate price and Adit was left alone without his confidante by his side.

Adit felt like he was dying inside. He'd lost his best friend to an act of violence and now he burned with a cold anger. No matter how hard he tried, no amount of money in the world could bring Nagbad back.

Adit began to unravel, going from village to village, killing and looting people mercilessly. People feared him, this mysterious figure that walked amongst them in the night. Yet Adit felt nothing - only emptiness as he fulfilled his newly found purpose for existence. On and on he carried his misery until one fateful day when he encountered another being just as hopeless as him.

It was another version of Babi Ngepet.

When Adit finally encountered this Babi Ngepet again, neither one of them said anything. They both knew what ended up happening—they had become two sides of the same coin—and all Adit could do was accept his fate and succumb to the same darkness that had consumed this person. In the end, it was Babi who raised his arm one last time and dealt the killing blow, ending Adit's reign of terror.

ΔΔΔ

Ghoul

It was a dark and stormy night somewhere in the Middle East. The sky was filled with thick, rolling clouds illuminated by bursts of lightning, creating an eerie and oppressive atmosphere. The sand of the desert was a deep black, whipped up by harsh winds and swirling around a group of soldiers who were on patrol, like a living force. The air was thick with the smell of rain and electricity, and the sounds of thunder echoed ominously throughout the night. The temperature dropped and the light became a charcoal gray, as spotted with dots of the blackest black, clustered on the streets and the rooftops, crawling and scuttling amongst the silences and the shapeless.

The stillness of the night was disrupted by an adolescent yell. The youngest soldier in the pack, Rabin, had shouted sarcastically, "What a time to be alive!" A couple of troops forced out subdued chuckles that reverberated through the darkness. A few veterans simply carried on as if they hadn't heard the remark. They had been around this place long before, having hearty laughs and making jokes, but their merriment eventually became scarce and their patience thinned.

Leading the patrol was Babar, who had witnessed it all. He had been cursed to this desolate expanse for more than six years now. "The things we do for God," he thought to himself while restraining his shifting thoughts from turning into screams. With a stern voice he screamed at Rabin: "Shut your mouth and stay alert. This isn't some campus or city you know, this is combat! We can joke back in camp."

Rabin opened his mouth ready to offer a biting retort but wisely checked himself and kept walking along in quiet obedience.

As they trudged through the desert sands, an eerily shrill scream rent the air, so chillingly loud that it throttled their breath. They frantically looked around in search of the source of this petrifying sound, but all seemed silent and shrouded in darkness. Suddenly, a distinct rustling noise jolted them out of their fear-stricken state and they spun around to find a dark figure galloping towards them with alarming speed. It was no enemy soldier, but something from the depths of their childhood nightmares - here alive and well before them.

The terror on their faces made it evident that they knew what this thing was - the unmentionable horror that had been whispered in hushed tones by their grandmothers - the Ghoul! Babar thought he had seen the worst of the worst; blood, gore, carnage...but he soon realized how wrong he was as his eyes fell upon this gruesome creature standing before them, sizing them up just like the ir enemies did earlier with pure abject fear. Nevertheless, Babar blinked harder to make sure he wasn't hallucinating and when the ghoul still remained he knew his worst nightmare had come true.

The ghoul had an eerie, almost skeletal appearance. Its sunken eyes glowed with a fiery red light and its long, bony fingers seemed to be permanently curled in a menacing gesture. Its skin was dark and withered, while its sharp, jagged teeth were visible from beneath its lips. It had a monstrous head, with long, wispy hair that seemed to move and coil as if it had a life of its own. It moved quickly and gracefully, like a phantom flickering through the night. The ghoul had an unpleasant stench of decay and death that filled the air around it. It smelled of sulfur, burning rubber, and bile that would make even the most hardened veteran like Babar gag.

Babar quickly regained his composure and finally screamed, "Shoot that bloody, ugly looking imbecile."

But the ghoul hurled itself from the mouth of the cave and bolted across the field toward a group of soldiers. It ran low to the ground, as if on all fours, and its long claws clawed up clumps of dirt as it dragged them through the grass. Its eyes glowed red with fury and its face bubbled with black blood. In one hand it held, what surely looked like a human skull. The soldiers quickly aimed their guns at the ghoul, but it moved with incredible speed and agility, evading their bullets. One soldier was caught off guard and was dragged into the darkness by the ghoul. The other soldiers could hear his screams echoing through the night.

They suddenly found themselves face to face with a bone-chilling realization. The enemy was no ordinary soldier, but an otherworldly creature, only spoken of in hushed whispers and legends. This ghoul had been causing terror throughout the land for weeks, devouring living beings, soldiers and civilians alike, without mercy or remorse. In a state of shock and disbelief, the troops glared at Babar. Rabin shouted through his tears directly into Babar's face, "So this is what you dragged us out here for? You said nothing about this being a suicide mission! How are we supposed to defeat this abomination? Is it even possible to drive it away - or will it devour us too? I'm only twenty years old; I have so many dreams that I haven't fulfilled yet."

Babar knelt down and cradled Rabin's chin in his hands. He gazed deep into Rabin's eyes and spoke slowly, "Rabin, I had no idea what we would find here today. You all know me; I'd never put any of you in harm's way knowingly." A chorus of affirmations drifted around them as they confirmed their faith in Babar's leadership. But still, their courage was nowhere near enough to overcome the terror of facing off against a supernatural entity.

Babar rose to his feet, the murky shadows stretching and warping around him. He met the eyes of his battle-hardened team, each one a skilled warrior in their own right. They looked to him for guidance, for a plan of action. The stakes were high - higher than ever before. There was no room for failure.

He took a deep breath and spoke with conviction, "I have faced down bombs, tanks, missiles, knives. I've seen humans turn into monsters on the battlefield; brothers going against brothers. It's not easy to watch your dreams burn in front of you. But I know there are people out there who need us."

The room fell silent as he paused.

"We're soldiers," he said quietly. "We signed up because we knew it wouldn't be easy. Because we believe in something greater than ourselves."

A murmur of agreement rippled through the group.

"We were born to protect the common people against any danger that befalls this great nation," Babar continued. "They didn't tell me how bad it would be, but I still marched on, knowing that somewhere a child can sleep peacefully, knowing that there are soldiers protecting them against harm."

He locked eyes with each member of his team, his voice rising in intensity.

"This might be our worst nightmare come true. But we're soldiers - we fight for what's right, we fight for those who cannot fight for themselves."

Electricity seemed to crackle in the air as each soldier stood up taller, more resolute.

"I was born a soldier and will die a soldier," Babar declared. "Who are we?"

A thunderous roar filled the room as they shouted in unison, "WE ARE SOLDIERS!"

They searched frantically, their hands moving fast as they rifled through boxes and shelves for weapons that would be effective against such a creature. The sound of metal clanking against metal filled the room. With each thud, they knew they were getting closer to what they needed. Finally, one of them let out a shout of triumph. They had found some silver bullets and fashioned some makeshift weapons using silver knives - jagged edges glinting in the dim light.

Their hearts raced with a mix of excitement and fear. They knew that this was their only chance to save themselves from the hideous monster that lurked outside. They sensed its presence just beyond them, pacing back and forth like a caged beast waiting to strike.

Carefully, they primed their weapons, holding them up to the light. It was clear that these crude implements weren't perfect or polished, but they were all they had.

They took one final breath before Babar faced them again. He wailed the battle cry again, "Who are we?"

But, he was not granted a response. The soldiers were frozen in fear as the ghoul suddenly materialized out of the shadows, pouncing upon Babar with lightning-quick reflexes and unrivaled ruthlessness. Try as they might, none among them possessed the power to move a muscle. They stood powerless, watching in terror as the beast tore Babar's head from his body and raised it high for all to see. Then came the most gruesome sight yet; as the Ghoul opened Babar's face wide, twisted its tongue inside and began to devour his eyes like a ravenous animal. Blood spilled everywhere.

Rabin screamed, "What a time to be alive!". He looked straight at the ghoul taunting it to come at him next. Rabin's courage was palpable in his stance as he stood defiantly in front of the ghoul. The ghoul seemed to take notice, towering over Rabin in an intimidating manner. Its teeth were razor-sharp and glinted in the dim light, a stark contrast to its boiling yellow eyes and thick black fur. Rabin's defiance brought the soldiers back from their stupor. The soldiers fought back with all their might, but the ghoul was too powerful for them. Rabin could hear the tearing of flesh and the sound of bones spurting blood. He saw the narrow eyed soldier sneaking up on the Ghoul. He saw weapons filled with flecks of blood as the soldier plunged them into his enemy. He smelled the iron from dead bodies and the sweat from the soldier. He tasted the smoldering flesh of the ghoul and the shiny silver knives. He felt the weight of the ghoul on the soldiers skin. He felt the bones splintering beneath the sharp teeth. He felt the heat of the blood spatter on his skin. He felt scared and he felt peace as the world around him faded away. It all became white like the colour in a photograph, when the camera flash bleaches out the rest of the colour in a picture. It was a colour that was not colour.

Rabin was the only one left standing, and his body quaked with rage. His comrades were strewn on the ground around him, yet his face held a steely resolve as he looked for ways to lure the ghoul into a trap. With a sweep of his arm, an iron circle of silver knives formed at his feet. The ghoul came closer and roared a final defiance in its death throes. Rabin flew towards it, plunging a knife deep into its heart. Its lifeless body collapsed onto the ground. In that moment, he knew there existed something darker than he could comprehend. He surveyed the carnage around him - it was once friends and allies that lay still in pools of their own blood. He would always remember this night; they had come face to face with an unspeakable terror.

Rabin wanted to leave and never come back. His head hurt, his muscles aching after the attack. He was packing his bags when all of the other villagers came around to thank him for saving them all. One by one they told their stories of the attacks that had happened in the night. He realised that it wasn't just one ghoul, there were many more. These ghouls were far more powerful than the one he had just defeated.

He felt the despair of knowing he was all that remained of his comrades as he vowed to avenge them. Fueled with rage and desperation, he devised a plan to track down the Ghoul pack and destroy them in their very own lair - a nearby cave. He no longer cared for himself or his own life, but with one last mission, he would make sure the Ghouls never terrorized anyone again. Wrapped in explosives, the determined warrior was ready to embark on a suicide mission, to take vengeance against the unholy creatures.

Rabin's feet felt heavy as he trudged up the rocky path towards the entrance of the cave. The howls and growling coming from within had his heart racing in terror. He stood at the mouth of the cave, steeling himself against the fear that threatened to overwhelm him. Taking a deep breath, he stepped inside to find a pack of ghouls eyeing him hungrily. As they launched toward him with a bloodcurdling screech, Rabin frantically tried to reach for the detonator in his pocket. With a loud boom and a flash of bright white light, in an instant, a tremendous explosion ripped through the cave, destroying everything within and sending shockwaves across the village.

The entire cave collapsed on top of the unsuspecting horde. A thick cloud of dust filled the air as twisted debris cascaded down upon them. All that remained of the once-thriving village was now a desolate wasteland, filled with nothing but devastation and sorrow; and stories of their terrifying deeds and Rabin's sacrifice were still told around campfires for many years afterwards.

$$\Delta\Delta\Delta$$

Asura

Thakur Dayal slammed his fists on the desk, his face twisted in anguish. His fingers dug into the wood of the desk, splintering and cracking it with each clench as a wave of agony flooded over him.

Dayal was a burly, older man, with a thick graying mustache and deep-set wrinkles from decades of hard work. Now retired, he still wore an old, tattered police uniform with a tarnished badge on his chest. The man was of medium build, with deep set eyes, a furrowed brow, and weathered skin that spoke of a lifetime of experience. His posture was strong and proud, even though he had no legs. His face was lined with stress and sadness, but his eyes were still determined and alert.

Dayal was born and bred in Rabale, his birthplace that had brought him solace and horror in equal measures. An idyllic village in western India, Rabale was surrounded by lush green hills and winding rivers. Small, terracotta-roofed houses dotted the landscape, with colorful sari-clad women and barefoot children walking through the streets. Brightly painted temples and shrines gave the town a festive atmosphere, and the smell of cooking fires and incense lingered in the air. The aroma of jasmine flowers drifted on the breeze, the air was filled with pungent spices from the local markets, along with fragrant flowers from nearby gardens. You could also smell earthy manure from the livestock, and a faint smoky scent from distant cooking fires. The peaceful sound of a thousand birds singing in unison filled the air, punctuated by the occasional braying of donkeys or the low hum of a distant motorbike. The clank of metal pots and pans could be heard from inside the homes as villagers prepared dinner while children laughed and played in the street.

Dayal had found his true love there and together, they had been blessed with two beautiful children. But it all changed when a maniac, Shabbar Singheshwar came to haunt their peace. Dayal's courage and strength enabled him to put an end to the man's evil deeds after many long years of suffering.

It still felt like yesterday to him, he had stumbled away from the smouldering wreckage of his home, an acrid stench of smoke and death heavy in the air. His heart felt like it had been ripped out of his chest, a constant reminder of the two warriors who had become his friends, only to be taken away in a single moment. He had lost everything - his wife, his children - but he found strength deep within himself as he made it his mission to protect the village. Taking on this mantle gave him purpose, and the villagers became his substitute family.

However, even that fight seemed like a walk in the park compared to what he faced now. For here was something far more powerful and insidious than any other wickedness he had ever encountered before. Something that left him feeling tiny and powerless against its might. Despite coming from a long line of warriors, Dayal felt defeated - like all hope was lost.

He remembered how it had all started, the hot summer night when he heard the whispers of a stranger on the wind. At first, it seemed like a dream, though one so captivating and real that Dayal could not help but be ensnared by its allure. But then came the reality: what began as whispers grew into an incessant chant, rising from a whisper until it roared like thunder across the land. The voice spoke of power, of strength and fear—of something dark and sinister that lurked just beyond the horizon and was slowly advancing toward them all.

When Dayal and the villagers finally laid eyes on the creature, they could scarcely believe what they saw. The creature was a hulking mass of muscle and fur, its body covered in thick black hair. Its face was twisted into an expression of perpetual malice, as if it had been burned in an inferno. Two red, glowing eyes pierced the darkness of the night, illuminated like fireflies in its fur-covered face. It had long sharp claws and four massive horns that extended from its head. Myths and legends had been whispered through their lives but never had they imagined that one day they would behold such a horrific sight in the flesh. Shrieks of fear and terror echoed through the air as nearly all of the village fled from the scene in a mad panic. Only a handful of brave souls remained including Dayal who withstood the shock as courage welled up within him, his heart hammering away in his chest. "What do you want?" He demanded of the beast, its red eyes burning into his own soul like embers set ablaze.

"You don't even ask my name," it retorted with an amused chuckle. "That is quite rude, yet your eyes tell me that you already know who I am. So I shall not waste time with these pesky small-talks." It declared before continuing menacingly, "I am the almighty Asura and what I seek is fresh blood; each Amavasya someone not more than five years old must be delivered to me by this very village. Negotiations are futile - only submission will spare your kin! Not complying with my demand will leave the young ones parentless, bastardized for eternity!"

The villagers were horrified at the thought of such an awful demand, but what choice did they have? Though terrified and panicked, Dayal knew that he had to do something. He gathered the bravest of the village's warriors and began to prepare for battle. Yet, as Amavasya approached, it became increasingly clear that no matter how well trained or brave they were, they wouldn't stand a chance against this monster. Dayal was desperate - he feared for his village and their future if Asura could not be defeated.

Just when all hope seemed lost, he remembered an ancient story passed down through generations of his people. A story about a powerful amulet that could cast away evil forces like Asura - though it had never been proven true until now. He quickly crafted one from clay and adorned it with symbols of protection and courage before setting off into the night in search of the beast along with his motley crew.

When Dayal finally found Asura again, he held up the amulet with trembling hands and whispered an old incantation under his breath as its power surged through his veins. To everyone's amazement, the creature vanished in a thick cloud of smoke!

But as the villagers were rejoicing in their newfound safety, Asura returned to the village bigger than ever. He charged right through the defensive wall that was put into place and killed all of the parents of five newborns and taunted Dayal, "You fool, if you ever try this again, I will destroy the village along with you." Many villagers died valiantly in battle while Dayal managed to escape by a narrow margin. The village council was terrified and decided to bow down to Asura's demands. Dayal was not fine with this, but his pleas were met with deaf ears.

"That's it," Dayal muttered to himself. "I must find allies who are powerful enough to defeat Asura." The task was urgent and required stealth; if the rest of the Council found out about his plans, he would be arrested or worse. Dayal paced back and forth in the small shack that was nestled into a hillside. His train of thought was interrupted when he heard movement outside. Thakur peered through a tiny window cut into the wood door. A huge man-like creature stood at the foot of the hill. He wore an animal skin over his bare chest, and around his neck was an array of colorful beads joined to one another by black string. His massive frame blocked the light from the setting sun, casting a dark shadow across the dirt road. Yeti looked straight into Thakur's eyes, conveying with one glance that he knew what was happening and that he understood his pain. Thakur went to the nearby mountain and called out to Yeti. He told Yeti about the terror Asura had wrought on his village and asked for his help. "Great Yeti, please help us! We need your strength and power to defeat Asura and save our village from further destruction," Thakur pleaded. Yeti, being an honorable creature, agreed to lend a hand. "I will help you, Thakur. Asura's reign of terror must end."

Thakur then, braved the haunted forests of Transylvania and

tracked down the infamous vampire Dracula. He had heard whispered stories of Dracula's immense power, and he knew that it was his only hope for saving his village from Asura, a demon of unspeakable strength. Despite Dracula's initial reluctance, Thakur begged desperately for his help. "Dracula! Please hear me out!" he shouted. "My home is under siege by an evil force, and we need your strength and cunning to defeat them!" With each word, Thakur's voice became more passionate, until finally Dracula was moved by his desperate plea and agreed to join his cause.

Dracula looked at Thakur for a moment, then spoke. "I am hesitant to involve myself in the affairs of mortals, but I can sense the sincerity in your words. Very well, I will help you." Together, the trio set out to take down Asura. They travelled to the village, and decided to bring out Asura in the guise of delivering the new born. The trio traveled silently through the night, their destination looming in the distance; a village surrounded by a wall of fear and despair. A lone figure, Dayal stood atop the hill, a beacon of hope against the shadows of evil. The trio made their way to the gates and entered the village, Thakur leading the way. The trio's footsteps echoed against the walls of the village, a solemn march into the unknown. The creaking of the gates marked their entrance, a resounding thud that spoke of danger.

Asura rose to his full height, an evil smirk stretched across his face. "Three of you against me? You're either brave or foolish," he taunted. Yeti lunged forward with a guttural roar, slamming into Asura and sending the demon careening backwards. Dracula descended from above, sharp fangs tearing at Asura's neck in a desperate attempt to subdue him. Asura screamed in agony before shaking Dracula off. He bared his teeth in rage, the air around him crackling with power. "You think you can win against me? I am unstoppable. Your futile attempts at victory are laughable!" Thakur stepped forward, resolute determination on his face. "No matter what form your power takes, we will overcome it. We will bring an end to your tyranny here and now."

Asura let out a wicked laugh that echoed throughout the valley. "You humans never cease to amuse me! If you think brute force alone can defeat me, you are gravely mistaken."

Thakur's voice was like a thunderclap when he shouted at the demon, "We have a secret weapon, Asura. We know your weaknesses, and we will use them against you!" Thakur unleashed a flurry of punches and shoulder pushes that had Asura reeling. Yeti and Dracula jumped in with their own special attacks. Asura fought desperately, but it was all for naught; the combined strength of the three heroes was too much for him. Finally, one last uppercut from Thakur sent the demon to the ground. The villagers erupted in cheers as the heroes emerged triumphant. They were enveloped by an adoring crowd that thanked them for saving the village.

Thakur bowed deeply, thanking Yeti and Dracula for their help. He could only hope that the three of them together had been enough to put an end to Asura's reign of terror. "It is done," he said, glancing at his companions as they made their way back home. Dracula nodded grimly. "Yes, and we have proven that even mortals can be powerful tools in the face of a common enemy." Yeti added hesitantly, "But I fear this may not be the last time we are called upon to defend our villages from such monsters."

As they trekked through the dismal landscape, Thakur fought back a wave of gratefulness that surged through him. Without his new allies, the defeat of Asura would have been a distant dream. He glanced at Yeti and Dracula in appreciation. "My heartfelt gratitude for your assistance," he said softly. Yeti gave a solemn nod. "We must consider it our duty to safeguard those who cannot protect themselves," rumbled Yeti. An agreement echoed by Dracula's gravelly reply, "And I must admit, it was quite thrilling to take down such a powerful foe. Perhaps we could do it again sometime." Thakur laughed. "I hope not, but I know that if we ever need to, I can count on you both." As they reached the base of the mountain, Yeti bid them farewell and headed back to his home.

Dracula's gaze bore into Thakur's with a fierce intensity. "Thakur, do not forget that Asura may be gone, but there are more hordes of darkness lurking in the shadows. Guard your village carefully, for they will seek to exploit even the slightest hint of weakness." Thakur nodded resolutely, his jaw set in determination. "I understand. I will remain vigilant and never let down my guard." Dracula reached out, gripping Thakur's shoulder firmly. "Remember, I am always here if you need me. You are not alone in this fight." A spark of courage flashed in Thakur's eyes as he felt the strength and warmth emanating from his friend. With newfound encouragement, Thakur watched as his ally parted and made his way into the night sky before heading back to his village filled with a fire that raged within him. He knew that with allies like Yeti and Dracula by his side, he could face anything that came his way.

Medusa

Long Long time ago, Medusa was the most beautiful woman ever. The legends said Medusa's hair was silver and her eyes were like emeralds. Her skin glowed and her lips were ruby red. Her face was sculpted like a goddess, her lips full, her eyes luminescent, her cheeks smooth. Her breasts were full, her nipples erect and ripe. She smelled like roses and peppermint. Her hair smelled of honey, and the grass she laid upon smelled of the perfume of the flowers that grew at her feet. Medusa's voice was soft and sweet like the song of a mourning dove. Her voice was quiet, like the sound of falling leaves. Her laughter was like the song of birds.

Few lucky men remembered, the taste of Medusa's lips was honey and nectar, a flavor as delicious as the finest of wines. The taste of her flesh was succulent and fresh.

But the goddess Athena cursed her for being too beautiful and turned her into a monster with snakes for hair. Medusa lived in a cave deep in the woods, away from civilization. The walls of the cave were jagged and uneven, filled with crevices that were home to small animals and birds. The floor was covered in dirt and rock. The ceiling was supported by large stones, and the cave was illuminated by soft moonlight that filtered through cracks in the walls.

In the darkness, Medusa's glimmering snakes stood out in stark contrast to the shadows around them. The cave was dark, but the glistening snakes on her head glowed in the moonlight. They looked like jewels, and their color changed from red to green to blue as they moved in time with Medusa's heartbeat. The scent of damp earth and moss pervaded the cave, with a slightly musty smell of wet stone. The freshness of the woods, with its smell of pine and cedar and moss, also lingered in the air.

Medusa was feared by all who knew of her, except for one man, the legendary hero Perseus. Perseus was tall and strong, with broad shoulders and a proud jawline. His hair was a dark chestnut, his eyes were a deep blue, and his skin was tanned from days in the sun. He was dressed in a suit of armor that glinted with gold and silver trim around the edges. His sword was masterfully crafted, with an ornate hilt and an edge that shone like moonlight in the night sky. The sound of Perseus's sword as it sliced through the air was crisp and clear. His footsteps were heavy yet light as he moved through the forests and caves, completing mission after mission. When he spoke, his voice was low but steady, with a hint of an ancient power that lingered beneath the surface.

Perseus was a brave man, and he was on a mission to slay the Gorgon, Medusa. He followed her trail from one cave to another, growing closer and closer to his target. As he ventured deeper into the woods, Perseus encountered creatures that had never been seen before. There were giant spiders with legs as big as tree trunks and boulder-sized eggs that cracked open with strange creatures inside of them. But none of these things scared Perseus; he felt a strength within himself that made him fearless. Finally, Perseus reached the entrance of Medusa's cave. He entered cautiously, wary of facing such an infamous monster. He heard an eerie noise coming from within the depths of the cave and knew it must be Medusa. His heart raced in anticipation as he drew his sword and stepped forward into the darkness.

Perseus crept along the walls of the cave, searching for any sign of the Gorgon. Finally, she appeared out of nowhere: a tall figure cloaked in shadows with glowing green eyes and a crown of writhing snakes atop her head. Her serpentine locks glistened in the moonlight, and her eyes sparkled like emeralds. He saw the monster up close, and he realized how beautiful she still was. She saw Perseus and hissed in rage before charging forward to attack him. Perseus had come prepared to fight the Gorgon, and he had his shield polished to a mirror-like finish. He caught a glimpse of Medusa in it, but he quickly looked away, for fear of falling under her spell. "You cannot defeat me, mortal," Medusa hissed, her snakes writhing angrily. "I will try," Perseus replied, his sword at the ready.

Medusa lunged at him, but Perseus sidestepped her attack and swung his sword. The blade struck her arm, but it did not harm her. Medusa laughed, and her laughter echoed through the cave. "You think you can harm me, mortal? I am immortal!" she taunted. Perseus fought desperately, his sword clashing aggressively against Medusa's. She was agile and quick, narrowly dodging each blow he threw at her. But she could feel the strength of his resolve, and it terrified her. "Why?" She asked meekly, taking a step back in surprise at her own voice. He paused for a moment, almost seeming to pity her. "I have been sent by the king of Argos. He wishes your head as a trophy." Tears welled up in Medusa's eyes. "Is it a crime to be beautiful? I am cursed by Athena, why must you take my life too?"

Perseus felt torn between his mission to slay Medusa, and the admiration for her power that he had begun to feel. He had never before encountered a creature like Medusa, who was both beautiful and deadly. Her eyes narrowed as she prepared to use her secret weapon, and terror filled Perseus' heart. He could sense an immense force emanating from her figure, one that rooted him to the spot and deprived him of his mobility. "What have you done to me?" Perseus asked, his voice strained with fear. "I have paralyzed you, Perseus. You cannot move until I release you." Medusa approached him slowly, as if he were a dangerous animal that might bite her. She could see the muscles in his body tensing and straining against the invisible bonds that held him. His fists clenched and unclenched, and he drew in deep breaths to steady himself. "You are a brave man, Perseus," she said, reaching out a hand to touch his face. "I do not want to cause you any pain."

Suddenly, Medusa's snakes began to writhe and hiss. Perseus felt a burning sensation on his face, and he realized too late what was happening. He closed his eyes, not wanting to see his own death. But nothing happened. Perseus opened his eyes and saw that Medusa was weeping. Her snakes had turned back into hair, and her face was once again that of a beautiful woman. "What has happened to me?" Medusa cried, looking at her hands in confusion. Perseus stood up, feeling no ill effects from the encounter. "I do not know, but it seems that Athena has lifted the curse." Medusa looked at him in disbelief. "You mean I am no longer a monster?" Perseus smiled. "It would seem so." Medusa wept tears of joy, and Perseus embraced her. The pair left the cave and stepped into the bright sunlight. The sun shimmered off of the trees and illuminated the vast landscape surrounding them. They walked side by side, their hands intertwined, and looked at each other with awe and admiration. Medusa was entranced by Perseus' handsome features and chivalry, and could feel her heart skip a beat as she looked into his eyes. The birds sang in the backdrop, creating a magical atmosphere of love and joy. It was a new beginning for both of them, and Medusa felt she had never met a man like Perseus before.

Together, their bodies moved with a passion that enveloped them both and seemed to ignite the room around them. Her pale skin, illuminated by the moonlight, glowed against his sun-kissed skin as they moved together in perfect harmony. Her hair cascaded down her back and over her shoulders in wild curls, while his hands brushed against her curves, tracing the outlines of her body. The pungent smell of love was thick in the air, mixed with a faint hint of roses and honeysuckle. The scent of desire was heightened by the sweet smell of their sweat, merging and intensifying their connection in an intoxicating way. Their tongues met in a passionate dance, exploring each other's mouths with a desperate hunger. Soft lips locked together in a tender embrace, and their cries of pleasure filled the room as they tasted each other's desire. Fingers tangled together as their bodies moved together in perfect harmony. Clothes were left forgotten on the floor as they explored each other's bodies. They made love like this for days.

Then suddenly as they were again kissing and making love, Medusa's snakes wrapped around Perseus, their sinuous forms curling around his body in a protective embrace. The snakes' eyes were glinting with a mysterious light and their scales were a deep green color. They moved with grace and agility, gliding over Perseus' skin with a slithering caress. Even as he struggled against them, he was mesmerized by their hypnotic movements.

The more he looked into her eyes, the more Perseus forgot who he was and why he had come there. He gazed into the brown fire of her irises as they shone like a pair of moons in the night sky. Medusa kissed Perseus all over, even the snakes wrapped around his body sent their poison deep into his body. He gasped in pain but was too enthralled by her beauty to break away. His eyes widened with surprise as he felt Medusa's tongue gently explore his neck and chest. She then traveled down his abdomen, leaving a trail of fire behind her lips. The snakes slithered along her body as she moved, their cold scales tickling his skin in a sensuous manner. They appeared to be almost guiding her movements as if they were one entity. The feeling was overwhelming and Perseus found himself lost in a strange world of pleasure and desire. As the venomous kisses continued, they began to have an effect on him, slowly numbing him to the pain and making him more pliable in Medusa's embrace. He felt like he was melting under her touch and becoming part of her being.

His head spun with a dizzying intensity as he felt himself surrendering completely to Medusa's passionate embrace and allowing his mind, body and soul to become one with hers. He closed his eyes and allowed himself to be taken over by the sensations her kisses evoked within him until he could no longer tell where hers ended and his began. Together they created an energy that bound them together like two halves of a perfect whole, each completing the other in perfect harmony.

The intensity of their connection was almost too much for Perseus to handle, but still he could not bring himself to break away from their blissful moment until eventually exhaustion set in and Perseus started convulsing and as the poison started circulating slowly in his blood, he started dying a slow and painful death.

Medusa stood up gracefully, her body swaying in time to her movements. She looked down at her victim and sneered, her eyes burning like embers with wicked delight. She reached out and ran a finger down the length of one of her snakes, and then looked back up as she said with a satisfied smirk, "One more for the Bad Girl."

$$\Delta\Delta\Delta$$

Mothman

The town of Point Pleasant was nestled in the hills of West Virginia. It was a sleepy little town, surrounded by lush green forests, rolling hills, and winding rivers. The streets were lined with old-fashioned buildings, from country stores and bakeries to churches and schools. In the evening, the sun sets over the town, painting it in a soft orange glow. The air in Point Pleasant was thick with the scent of wildflowers and freshly cut grass. In the evenings, you could smell the woodsmoke from distant fireplaces and bonfires. On hot summer days, you could catch whiffs of hickory and cherry from the local barbeques.

The town was alive with the sound of chirping birds, buzzing bees, and rustling leaves. In the evening, you could hear crickets singing in harmony and cicadas singing their evening lullaby. At night, it was quiet but not eerie; an occasional dog barking or owl hooting filled the silence just enough to be comforting. She was a sparse, spartan place - a town tightened by the disappearing of the river and kept alive only by the people whose homes were built on the broken banks of what might once again swell wide.

Here lived Thomas, a hardworking man with an honest face and a strong build. His clothes were simple but sturdy, and his hands were rough from the hard labor of farming. He wore a wide-brimmed hat to protect his face from the sun and a pair of old boots that had seen better days. Thomas had the faint smell of freshly cut grass and sweat, as he often spent his days working in his fields. His voice was low and gentle, but there's a strength to it that could be heard in the timbre of his words. He walked with purpose, his boots thudding against the ground as he strode through his fields.

But one night, Thomas's life changed forever. He was out in his fields, inspecting the crops when a chill ran down his spine as he heard an unfamiliar noise coming from the woods. He trudged closer and saw a figure shrouded in darkness, its eyes glowing an eerie yellow. It appeared as a humanoid figure, shrouded in darkness and wearing a hood that concealed its face. Its wings were large and powerful, beating with a muted thunder as it moved. Its eyes were bright yellow and they seem to burn with an unnatural light. Its movements appeared graceful, almost as if it were floating on air. It carried with it a scent of decay and death, like an old graveyard that had been forgotten for centuries.

"Who are you?" asked Thomas, shaking uncontrollably. It spoke with a deep, menacing tone, its words vibrating through the air like thunder and each syllable emanating power. Its wings beat furiously as it flew around, creating a loud whooshing sound as it moved through the air. "I am the Mothman," replied the mysterious figure.

Fear raced through Thomas's body as he had never heard of such a thing before. The creature spoke in a deep, menacing tone: "I have come to warn you Thomas; evil is coming to this town, and you must be ready."

The Mothman spoke in a somber tone that left no room for doubt - deep danger lurked nearby. Refusing to take any chances, Thomas broke into a run back to his house, hoping he wasn't too late to warn his family. When he arrived panting for breath, his family were dubious about what he said. "You must be seeing things," they told him, but secretly they feared it was true. Sure enough, strange events began taking place all around town - disappearances of people who had gone out into the night and never returned; sightings of shadowy figures where none had been before; and eerily-guttural sounds that seemed to whisper something dire just beyond their hearing.

His family knew that Thomas hadn't been mad after all - this was something from another world... something that could not be stopped. It wasn't long before fear began to spread through the streets like wildfire. Everyone was on edge all of the time, afraid of what might be lurking in the shadows. Businesses closed early and children were kept indoors for fear of what could possibly be out there in the darkness. Even the bravest amongst them were wary of venturing too far beyond their homes after nightfall.

As the months went by, Thomas became obsessed with the Mothman, spending all his time trying to uncover the creature's secrets. Thomas was seen talking to people all around town, asking questions and listening intently. He had a determined look in his eyes, as if he was looking for something that he could not find. He would talk to anyone willing to listen, but sadly no one had any answers for him.

And then, one night, the air was still and humid as Thomas felt the presence of something sinister before he caught sight of it. The Mothman descended from the sky, its red eyes glowing with a dangerous intensity. Its wings beat furiously against the wind, and a sound like thunder echoed through the town.

"Thomas," it boomed, "you have done well, but now it is time for you to pay the price." Its claws grasped his arms as it launched into a violent attack. Thomas attempted to fight back, but he was no match for the creature's overwhelming strength. He crumbled to the ground, battered and bruised, his mind shattered by the horror of what he had seen. But inexplicably, the Mothman left him alive. As Thomas lay there in pain, he knew that speaking about the Mothman had made it more powerful and dangerous.

Months passed since Thomas's encounter with the Mothman. The town of Point Pleasant had become a ghostly landscape with small clusters of people scurrying inside homes, the only sound being their hurried footsteps and hushed whispers. The streets were empty, and the air was heavy with tension, as if something ominous was lurking in the shadows. Signs of fear and paranoia were everywhere, from boarded-up windows to hastily-erected security systems. People had locked themselves inside their homes, afraid to venture out at night. The strange occurrences were becoming more frequent, and nobody knew what was causing them.

Thomas's face was pale and drawn, with dark circles under his eyes from lack of sleep. He had grown gaunt from not eating, his clothes were unkempt, and his expression was haunted. He kept to himself, rarely speaking to anyone and avoiding contact with anyone who might try to help him. He constantly scanned the shadows for any sign of the Mothman's return. He couldn't shake off the feeling that the creature had left something unfinished.

The night was hot, and Thomas had finally managed to doze off with the window open. He awoke to the sound of pounding at his front door, like a fist beating against his walls. He sat up and listened carefully. As the knocking continued, he grew more and more uneasy, but the noise did not cease. When he finally mustered the courage to look outside, he saw the Mothman standing on his porch. The creature's leathery wings beat slowly as it stared down at him with its red eyes. "Thomas, I need your help," said the creature, its voice barely above a whisper. "There is something much bigger at play here, and I need you to help me stop it."

Thomas stared at the creature and wondered if he was hallucinating. It made sense that something like this would happen after all of the stress he had been under lately. But was there really something much bigger at play here? Could the universe get any stranger than this?

Thomas was skeptical but curious. To his own astonishment, he stepped outside, and the Mothman handed him a piece of parchment. On it was a map with a strange symbol marked in the center. "What is this?" asked Thomas. "It's a portal to another realm," replied the Mothman. "Something is trying to break through, and we must stop it before it's too late." Thomas looked at the Mothman with suspicion. "Why should I trust you? You attacked me last time." "I had to test you," replied the creature. "I needed to see if you were worthy of the task ahead. And now, I see that you are."

Thomas was still unsure, but he knew that he had to do something to save his town. He followed the map to the location of the portal. A group of dark, hooded figures surrounded the portal in a circle, their cloaked bodies creating an imposing wall of darkness. They were chanting in a strange language Thomas had never heard before. It sounded like a mixture of Latin and something else he couldn't identify. The air around the portal seemed to crackle with energy, and an eerie glow emanated from the figures' hands. The portal itself seemed to glow with a mysterious light, beckoning Thomas closer. Thomas' eyes fell upon the dreaded sign on the parchment, and he knew his time was short. In haste, he snatched up a scrap of paper and feverishly began sketching the menacing symbol. Suddenly, from out of the shadows emerged the hooded figures with swords in hand. Without hesitation, Thomas bravely rose to meet the challenge, yet sadly his strength was not enough to overcome their numbers. A merciless fight ensued.

Thomas held his breath as a wave of fear washed over him, and suddenly, the ominous figure of the Mothman emerged from the darkness. He exhaled with relief, yet remained paralyzed in terror as he looked upon the legendary creature.

But instead of helping him, the creature turned on him, its wings beating furiously as it attacked. Thomas tried to defend himself, but he was no match for the creature's strength. As he lay dying, he heard the Mothman speak to him one last time. "You were the key, Thomas. You were the only one who could stop them. And now that you're gone, they will be unstoppable." And with that, the Mothman flew away, leaving Thomas to die alone.

As it turned out, the hooded figures were a cult trying to summon an ancient demon from another dimension. The Mothman had warned Thomas because he needed his help to stop the cult. But then the Mothman realised that the cult was actually worshiping him. And when Thomas became the only one who could stop them, the

Mothman realized that he had to eliminate him to ensure the cult's success.

The Mothman initially warned Thomas about the danger that was coming to Point Pleasant, hoping that he would be able to stop it. However, Thomas became obsessed with the Mothman and spent all his time trying to uncover its secrets. This inadvertently led to the formation of the cult, who believed that the Mothman was a deity that could protect them from the impending disaster. The Mothman realized that the cult's belief in a demon from another realm was dangerous and could lead to their demise. The cult members demanded power over the universe, but their willful ignorance would lead to their destruction.

It saw Thomas as a threat to the cult's belief system, but then it attacked him to silence him and ensure the cult's success. In its eyes, Thomas was just one of many sacrifices that would lead Point Pleasant on the road to destruction. The Mothman's warning was sincere, but it never intended for humans to worship it. When Point Pleasant fell under misfortune, the Mothman felt responsible for exacerbating these issues. In the end, the Mothman's actions brought about the very disaster it had warned Thomas about, and the town of Point Pleasant was left to suffer the consequences of the Mothman's wrath.

ΔΔΔ

Jorogumo

A fishing village was nestled deep in the lush forest of Japan, surrounded by towering cedar trees, lush pine, and blossoming hinoki cypress. The village was quaint and peaceful, with wooden shacks built along the riverside and cobblestone streets leading up to a small temple. A faint glow of lanterns and the sound of crickets in the night filled the air.

The scent of saltwater, seaweed, and fish hung heavily in the air, with thick plumes of cooking smoke rising from chimneys. There was also a faint smell of incense, left behind by those who seek blessings from their ancestors before they set sail into the unknown.

The villagers could be heard singing old fishing songs as they mend their nets and repair their boats, while local merchants hawk their wares with bright smiles and boisterous conversations. There was also a faint sound of wind whistling through trees, and a subtle hum from the harbor as ships came in.

In the village spread across the centuries, the legend of Jorogumo. Jorogumo was said to be a beautiful woman with long, dark hair and piercing green eyes. But under her skin, eight spider legs sprout from her back, vibrating with an eerie clicking sound. The spider woman smelled of death and decay, like a forgotten tomb or a rotting corpse. Her presence was like a foul stench that lingered in the air - a reminder of the victims she has claimed for her own.

Jorogumo had an unsettling voice, soft and faint like a whisper in the wind. Stories said, It lulled the men in an eerie trance, as if she were beckoning them to come closer to her web. When she spoke, her words were like the hiss of a snake, her threats and promises chilling their bones. When she touched her victims, it was like being pricked by a thousand needles all at once. Her fingers were cold and slimy, crawling across their skin as if trying to find the sweetest are of their skins. She had very long arms, silver as eels on those nights, and armpits as dark and mysterious as sea urchins.

It was said that she sat at the mouth of the river, waiting for the unwary fisherman to approach her. Her spiderweb arms would envelop him and slowly tighten around him until he drowned in the waters from which he drew his living.

One night, a group of fishermen sat around a campfire, trading stories and drinking sake. They laughed and joked, enjoying their time together. As the night progressed, the fishermen grew bolder and the stories began to get wilder. One man, an old fisherman with a long white beard and a scar over his eye, regaled the group with a tale about Jorogumo. He spoke of her beauty and her power, of how she could ensnare her victims in an unbreakable web of fear.

"She is no ordinary spider," he said with a grimace, "but a being from another world." The other men listened attentively as he went on to describe how she would lure unsuspecting fishermen into her web with her mesmerizing voice and wicked charms.

Fearful yet curious, the men decided to test their courage by venturing out into the dark waters to look for the spider woman. They rowed their boats silently through the murky depths and were soon met with an eerie sight: multiple webs suspended in midair like strange veils that reached out towards them, glinting menacingly in the moonlight.

As he looked down, the other men watched in shock as a black spider scuttled up the length of his pants. He brushed it away with trembling fingers, but the sickening feeling only seemed to grow worse. It spread throughout his body like a venomous fog, wrapping itself around his throat and squeezing until he could no longer gasp for air. The other men watched frantically as the color drained from his face and he began to tremble wildly. They saw the venomous toxin spread throughout his body like wildfire, clawing at every inch of his being.

The men stood there, unable to move, as a figure emerged from the shadows at the far end of the room. She was beautiful - almost too beautiful to be real - her long dark hair cascaded in waves around her shoulders and her green eyes peeked from beneath thick lashes. But as she approached them, their terror only grew when they realized that a set of eight grotesque spider legs protruded from her back, twitching and writhing like tentacles.

"Help me," the man croaked, gasping for breath. Jorogumo appeared before him, her eyes filled with a sinister glee. "I can help you," she purred, "but only if you do something for me." The man nodded, desperate for relief from his anguish. "Anything," he uttered through gritted teeth. Jorogumo gestured to the other men, her voice dripping with malice. "Bring me one of them," she commanded. The man stared in horror at her demand, knowing what he had to do. He steeled himself and pointed shakily at one of his friends, and Jorogumo descended upon them like a hawk upon its prey.

The other men watched in terror as the figure of the woman shrouded their friend in a thick, black web, trapping him in her cruel embrace. The man's body was still, his eyes closed as if in a peaceful slumber. But then, her jaw opened wide, exposing a set of sharp fangs that glistened with venom. She sank them into his neck and the man's body began to wither away, becoming nothing more than a dried-up husk.

The sound was deafening - a piercing shriek echoing through the air that made the men tremble. It was like the screams of a thousand tortured souls, all rolled into one. But then came the worst sound of all - the sickening slurp of venom being sucked from their friend's neck. This was followed by a ghastly silence that seemed to last an eternity until finally, there was nothing left of him but a lifeless corpse.

And then, Jorogumo turned to them, a wicked smile on her face. "Now, who's next?" she asked.

The rest of the fishermen finally woke up from their shock and awe. The men had a plan. The men reached into their pockets and pulled out a small talisman, a round disc made of bronze with intricate etchings and symbols. It shone brightly in the moonlight, seemingly almost alive with energy.

As Jorogumo advanced on them, they held up the talisman, chanting ancient prayers. As the men chanted, the talisman gave off a low hum that grew louder and more intense with each passing second. Eventually, it began to buzz and vibrate with an otherworldly energy that filled the air around them. They could feel its power coursing through their veins, giving them hope and courage in the face of Jorogumo's evil intent.

And to their surprise, it worked. Jorogumo screeched in pain as the talisman burned her skin, forcing her to retreat back into the darkness. The men breathed a sigh of relief, grateful to be alive. They had already lost one of their own and wanted to reach back to the safety of their villages as quickly as possible.

The group of fishermen made the long trek back to the village, but something was off. Their dear friend and companion who had suggested bringing the talisman with them was nowhere to be seen, and a terrifying realization crept in - he'd gone missing. A deathly silence filled their minds as they looked around for a sign of him, and then an eerie sound cut through their despair. Chittering and clicking echoed from all directions, each getting louder and closer until it seemed to be coming from everywhere at once. Their blood ran cold as they saw her emerge from the shadows - Jorogumo, with their missing friend writhing helplessly in her web. They knew that none of them would survive if they attempted to fight her, so they held still and silently prayed that their lost ally might somehow make his own escape.

Suddenly, an answer came in the form of a chittering and clicking noise echoing from all directions, getting louder and closer until it seemed to be coming from everywhere at once.

It was the sound of hundreds of spiders - an entire swarm converging on Jorogumo. She screeched in rage as the swarm surrounded her, trying desperately to protect herself but ultimately failing against their overwhelming numbers. The spiders bit into her flesh and tore apart her webbing until there was nothing left but a pile of twitching limbs and tattered cloth on the ground.

And when the chaos died down, their missing friend burst forth from underneath the pile - alive! He ran back to where the group stood speechless, embracing each man with tears in his eyes before collapsing into their arms from exhaustion.

The men thanked whatever gods had intervened on that fateful night, for without their help....their dear friend would most definitely be dead now.

They decided then and there never to venture out alone again; they knew they'd need one another if they hoped to survive future encounters with Jorogumo or any other evil that lurked outside the village walls. From then on, no man would ever go it alone again - not while his friends were by his side!

ΔΔΔ

Aswang

A small village nestled in the mountains of the Philippines, with terracotta tiled roofs that glint in the sun and bright colors adorning houses made of stone and wood. Stretching far on either side were endless fields of wild grass and wildflowers that sway with each breeze. The sun setting behind the mountain range painting a beautiful orange hue across the sky. The scent of freshly baked bread wafted through the air, mixing with the smell of wildflowers that grew in abundance around the village. When it rained, you could smell the earthy musk of damp soil mingled with wood smoke from nearby homes. The sound of cicadas and songbirds filled the air, along with the rustling of the leaves in the wind, and the occasional bark of a distant dog. The river that flew just outside of the village town limits could be heard gurgling and bubbling, providing a soothing background noise.

But the village was slowly turning into a modern town. A construction site... cinder blocks and steel beams, mud and dried gravel, concrete mixers and bobcats, bricks and mortar and hard hats, machines and cranes and vans, a fireman and his yellow truck, men and women, men and men and men and women, metal pipes and polyurethane, spark arrestors and Y-connectors, pulley systems and gasoline, metal studs and nylon rope and air conditioning units, the blue crane, a metal wheel and some red bricks, boots and bullets and pins, a carousel and a curve, a saw and a shadow, a swirl and a wheel, a wheel and a mill, some cocoa, some lips, a kiss, a bit of light, a spool of ribbon, a women and a man, a man, a man and a woman, a man, a bit of light and a twist, a gloss, some fuzz, a man and a woman, a man, a man and a woman.

The city had been transformed with the passage of time, yet despite the modernization, people still cowered in fear of the Aswang. Legends persisted and whispered stories traveled from one person to another, passing on the frightful tales of the mythical creature that lurked within the shadows.

According to Legends, the Aswang was a mythical creature that roamed the streets at night, preying on anyone it could find. The Aswang was a monstrous creature with a long, serpentine body and four limbs. Its eyes glow bright red, and its mouth was filled with sharp, razor-like teeth. Its skin was leathery and scaly, shifting between shades of gray and black. The Aswang was said to have a thick miasma of rotten eggs, animal musk and decaying flesh that hung in the air around it. It smelt like death itself, as if it had just crawled out from the depths of hell.

The Aswang's movement was silent but deadly. People said its presence was marked by a low, guttural growl, a menacing rumble that rolls through the air like thunder. It hissed and snarled, its claws scraping against the ground as it moved. Its breath was a deep and sinister whisper, a wind of dread that sent chills down its victims' spines. It was red-skinned, bursting with muscles and bulging with veins. It had a long, thin head with a large mouth and sharp teeth, and its eyes were narrow and thin. It had a large nose, bulbous and purple, and its ears, which were small and fleshy, looked like the fins on a sunfish. It had a short, squat body that was always damp, and a thick stinger dangled beneath it like a long tail. Finally, it had a long, thin tongue that darted in and out of its mouth.

What struck fear into the hearts of all who encountered it was its ability to transform itself, taking on the most sinister shape of all - that of a human. In the dead of night, it would creep up on unsuspecting victims, baring long razor-sharp claws which it would then use to tear them limb from limb.

Rabi was a petite young woman who lived in the village. She had delicate features and wide, almond-shaped eyes. Her dark hair was in a long braid that fell over her shoulder and down her back. Her skin was pale, almost translucent, and she wore a simple dress of white linen. The village was peaceful, a tranquil haven for the people who lived there. But Rabi's presence was marked by gentle laughter and kind words, her voice an inviting whisper that spread compassion and joy.

Rabi felt her unborn child stir within her, and fear coursed through her veins like icy water. She was about to become a single mother, facing the unknown with courage - though she could not quell the dread that threatened to consume her every thought. Memories of her grandmother's feared tales of the Aswang came rushing back, and in the darkness of night she was haunted by visions of a fearsome creature that had once taken away her beloved sister. Every time the wind rustled outside the window, terror gnawed at Rabi's heart, and still she had never seen the Aswang up close.

One night Rabi had to venture out of her home and into the forest to find food. Rabi's feet carried her through the starless night, the void of darkness an oppressive force. With each anxious step, her breath grew shallow as she scoured the blackness for any sign of danger. Then, from behind, a sound like parchment being crumpled filtered through the air and froze Rabi in her tracks. A chill ran down her spine as a thousand eyes it seemed descended upon her from the shadows. She stood still as death, too scared to move, as the noise grew ever louder.

Rabi had just spun around when the Aswang launched itself at her. She screamed in agony as its jagged claws tore into her flesh, shredding it like tissue paper. Her legs gave way beneath her, and she tumbled onto the ground, gasping for breath. Fear overwhelmed her as she realised that sheer terror was no match for the unworldly strength of the Aswang. With every ounce of hope she had left, Rabi silently beckoned to any deity who might lend their assistance. All seemed lost as the Aswang stood looming over her like a piece of nightmarish art, ready to end her life.

Suddenly Rabi's stomach lurched, her unborn child sending a jolt of energy through her body. The Aswang gave a start, taken aback by the burst from within Rabi's swollen womb. She felt another kick and then another in rapid succession - her baby fighting for its life. In that moment she could feel the strength of a million mothers, the power of nature itself bursting from within her. Rabi saw her opening and lunged at the creature, a wooden stake clenched in her fingers. She made it to within inches of the Aswang's heart before it could react, but her aim was true, and she drove the stake home through unfeeling flesh into the cold, empty organ. The Aswang's scream ripped through the atmosphere, cutting off abruptly as it slammed backward into the trees behind them. Rabi leaned forward and spit on the creature's body.

The Aswang lay crumpled on the ground, its body motionless and cold. Its eyes no longer held the malice that they once did, instead only a dead stare is left in their place. Rabi lay next to it, trembling and weak. Her breaths came in shallow rasps as she struggled for air. Her pale face was contorted with pain and her clothes were stained red with her blood.

Few villagers found her but it was too late. But not for her son. Rabi lay on the ground, her body exhausted from the effort of giving birth. Her skin was pale and her clothes were stained with blood. A few villagers were standing around her, their faces filled with shock as they realized it was too late to save her. But nestled in her arms was a beautiful baby boy, his skin glowing in the moonlight and his eyes wide with wonder. Tears streamed down her pale face as she took in the sight of her boy and kissed his forehead one last time, before her life faded away.

The villagers raised him as one of thier own, naming him Anak-Rabi. He was tall, with dark hair and bright eyes that shone with determination. He had strong broad shoulders and muscular arms. His dark hair was cropped close to his head, and his bright eyes glistened with determination. His skin practically glowed in the moonlight, a testament to the courage of his mother and all that she gave up for him. The villagers could see that he had never forgotten his mother's bravery and they were proud to call him one of their own.

Anak-Rabi trained relentlessly, honing his body and mind. He practiced martial arts and swordplay, and exercised diligently. He was tireless in his pursuit of perfection, his muscles rippling with energy and his eyes burning with focus. He would use anything at his disposal to prepare for his mission - seek and eliminate each and every Aswang in the village, sacrificing sleep and leisure to perfect his technique. His movements were graceful and powerful, as if he could anticipate every move the Aswang would make. He was prepared for anything, his eyes glowed with a feverish intensity; they burned with power, the same power that drove him relentlessly through the forests, through the thick underbrush and spider webs, through the shadows and the moonlight, through the thorns and branches, through the animals and the skeletons, through the tar and the acid, through the flames and the molten rocks, through the clouds and the wind. What burned inside him was not the candle of life but the tireless fire of vengeance. Inside he his heart blazed brighter than a dozen suns. He ran through the hell of his heart and a sweat of determination poured from his every pore. He could almost feel his heart purify itself, firing on all cylinders for the sake of revenge.

Anak-Rabi was shrouded in darkness, illuminated only by the light of the full moon and the stars. He was walking quickly, nimbly making his way through the dense vegetation and thick underbrush of the forest. He was focused, his eyes darting from side to side as he searched for his target. He had been tracking this Aswang for days and tonight he knew he will find it. He walked into a clearing, where he finally spotted his quarry, sitting in a bar surrounded by unsuspecting villagers. He slowly approached, ready for anything.

The Aswang recognized him immediately. The malevolent creature lunged at him, talons flashing like quicksilver in the moonlight. He felt a rush of cool air as he leapt aside, barely avoiding its slashing claws. A surge of righteous fury surged through him and in one swift motion he spun to his right, driving his open hand into the monster's jaw with enough force to make it stumble back with a muffled cry. The Aswang regained his balance quickly and lunged at him again, like a hawk stooping upon a field mouse. His black claws that were long, shining and as sharp as a razor. He stood at the ready, his face as dark as a moonless night. The dark folds of his skin glimmered as he trembled. His entire being quaked with anticipation, like an elk on the eve of the rut.

The fight was intense and unrelenting. Both the man and the Aswang had a manic energy, their movements were swift and precise. The Aswang would lunge one moment, then dodge an attack from Anak the next. Sweat dripped from both of them as they fought, their clothing becoming more and more disheveled with each exchange of blows. Sparks occasionally leapt from their weapon as they clashed, and each combatant's breath was laboured as they tried to outlast the other.

Anak's years of training had given him a razor-sharp focus, but the Aswang's strength and agility were formidable. Finally, after what seemed like hours of fighting, Anak saw his chance. The Aswang made a fatal mistake, leaving itself open to a decisive blow. The man delivered a powerful kick to the creature's chest, sending it flying backward. The Aswang let out a final, guttural scream and fell to the ground, dead. The man stood over the creature's lifeless body, panting heavily. He shed a tear for his mother, knowing that he had avenged her death but this was just the beginning. He cannot stop until the last Aswang was destroyed.

ΔΔΔ

Zmei

The Carpathian Mountains rose up like a fortress, their jagged peaks piercing the sky like spearheads. Ancient forests line the base of the mountains, lush and verdant with towering trees and undiscovered creatures. Rays of golden sunlight filtered through thick clouds, illuminating the rocky terrain and cascading waterfalls. The Mountains had a distinct smell, of fresh pine needles and crisp mountain air. It was a scent that was both invigorating and calming, like a cool breeze on a hot summer's day. They were alive with the sound of rustling leaves and chirping birds, a chorus of singing insects that filled the air with a gentle hum. The stones in the Carpathian Mountains were unforgiving and rough, their edges sharp like broken glass. A misstep could lead to an unfortunate tumble down the steep slopes, where one can get lost amidst the treacherous terrain.

Here, a group of hikers stumbled upon a cave system that they had never seen before. Excited at the prospect of exploring uncharted territory, they made their way down the winding tunnels. The group of hikers consisted of five friends, Alex, Macey Mark, Lisa, and John. They were an array of diverse personalities. Alex stood tall and confident, with a mischievous sparkle in her eye and a mop of unruly black hair. Macey was the impulsive one, always jumping at the chance for adventure. Mark was the logical one, always weighing out their options before making a decision. Lisa was the quiet one, content to observe and assess the situation before speaking. John was surely the leader, strong-willed and determined to make sure they all pass this adventure with flying colors.

The cave entrance was hidden beneath a thick thicket of ivy, its entrance shrouded in a veil of emerald leaves. As the hikers pushed their way through, they discovered a sprawling network of winding tunnels, illuminated by an eerily faint light. The walls of the cave were damp and jagged, reaching towards each other as if in a silent embrace. The air was heavy and stale, as if nothing had breathed it in for centuries. A shiver ran through the group as they felt the weight of history in the air.

The deeper they went, the darker and more silent the cave became. They stopped occasionally to catch their breath and marvel at their surroundings. Stalactites hung from the ceiling like icicles and stalagmites grew from the ground like frozen fingers. Bats flew around in circles above their heads while glowworms provided patches of light in between the shadows.

But as they progressed further into what seemed like an endless tunnel system, a chilling feeling began to take hold of them all. It was as if something sinister lurked just out of sight-something waiting patiently in the darkness for its chance to strike. The atmosphere became thick with tension and fear as they kept moving forward despite their instincts telling them otherwise.

Finally, after what felt like hours spent navigating down narrow passageways and up steep inclines, they emerged into an expansive cavern filled with ancient stone structures and mysterious symbols carved into its walls. The five friends looked on in awe; this place had clearly been untouched for centuries yet somehow it felt strangely familiar to all of them. Was this place part of some forgotten civilization? What secrets did these walls hold?

As they delved deeper into the earth, they heard a faint hissing sound that grew louder with each step. Suddenly a massive serpent slithered out of the darkness, its scales reflecting a faint glimmer in the dim light. It had a long, sinuous body that coiled around itself like a spring, its scales an earthy green with tinges of silver and gold. Its eyes were a smoldering yellow-orange, watching the hikers carefully as it hissed at them. The serpent hissed and rattled with each movement, a menacing sound that echoed through the caverns. Its claws scraped against the stone ground with each step, adding a sharp staccato to the atmosphere.

The hikers trembled in fear as the beast coiled around them, squeezing and trapping them in an ironclad grip. Every muscle in their body twitched and tightened as they felt the cold breath of death pressing against their faces.

It was a Zmei, an ancient dragon-like creature of Slavic mythology that had been lying dormant for centuries. The Zmei was an imposing creature, with a long, sinuous body that coils around itself like a spring. Its scales were an earthy green with tinges of silver and gold, reflecting a faint glimmer in the dim light. Its eyes were a smoldering yellow-orange, watching its prey eagerly. Its claws were sharp and curved, and its tail is tipped with a sharp spike. The Zmei's breath reeked of sulfur and burning embers, a reminder of its deadly fire-breathing capabilities. Its body exuded a musky scent that was vaguely reminiscent of the deep sea.

It was covered in hair, and it smelled like old fish and dried saliva. Its giant black hands were leathery and rough, and it had a voice like a sigh. Its hair was greasy, and its razor-sharp teeth were yellow and loose. Its claws were green and disturbing, pulsating like moldy shaving cream mixed with blood. It had thick horns on its head, sniffing the air with its crooked, ear-less nose. Its belly was hairy and wrinkly, and it had tiny cloven hooves the size of nickels. It had a tail that matched its hands and feet, covered in dark matted hair that was squirming and twitching. Its body was shaped like a pair of prunes, sticking out of its neck like warts, and one of its eyes was silver and dead and the other was a bright yellow lemon. It was old.

The Zmei unleashed an unholy roar that shook the very earth and sky, its sharp claws and barbed tail brushing aside any obstacles in its path. With a single sniff, it could pick up the faintest scent of its prey, driving it forward with an unquenchable bloodlust. Its teeth shone like stars as it opened its maw wide and unleashed a searing inferno that reduced anything in its way to ash. One by one, the hikers started getting torn apart by the creature's razor-sharp claws and incinerated with its hellish breath.

Alex was the first to go. He had strayed too far from the others, and by the time they found him, it was too late. Alex's lifeless body was sprawled on the ground, his limbs twisted in unnatural angles and his clothes stained with blood. His clothes were shredded and his skin torn and burned, scarred from the creature's deadly claws.

Macey was next, In the grip of the Zmei, its razor-sharp claws and barbed tail gripping her tightly. Her clothes were shredded, and her skin was torn and burned from its powerful claws. Her screams echoed through the caverns, The Zmei's powerful jaws clamped down on Macey's chest, tearing apart her skin and flesh as it greedily chewed and swallowed her. Blood spewed from her wound while she screamed in agony, her limbs flailing as the Zmei ripped her apart. The Zmei devoured Macey with an animalistic hunger, and the smell of seared flesh, warm blood, and charred skin filled the air as it gorged on her.

Mark, Lisa, and John were all alone in the forest, feeling hopeless and scared. As they quivered together, they heard the menacing hiss of the Zmei drawing near. They knew that their chances of survival were slim, but they still held onto a sliver of hope as it moved closer.

The three of them ran for their lives, desperately trying to outrun the Zmei. As they ran, John remembered a story his grandmother had told him about how to kill the Zmei. He knew that it was their only chance at survival, so he quickly relayed it to Mark and Lisa.

Mark and Lisa listened intently as John explained the plan. Knowing that this was their only way out, they agreed without hesitation. The three of them split up and ran in different directions, hoping to distract the Zmei long enough for John to carry out his plan.

The Zmei was relentless in its pursuit of its prey, but Mark and Lisa managed to keep it busy long enough for John to find what he needed.

He found a rock deep within the forest with strange symbols etched into it that his grandmother had told him about in her stories. Taking a deep breath, he grabbed the rock and rushed back towards the others as fast as he could go.

John threw the rock onto the ground near where Mark and Lisa were being chased by the Zmei. Immediately, there was an explosion of light that blinded everyone in its wake-including the Zmei-momentarily paralyzing it in place while allowing Mark and Lisa enough time to escape before it regained its senses again.

The mysterious rock appeared to have magical properties and when the Zmei had been paralyzed, it was as if time itself had stopped. They were completely safe-it seemed that their plan actually worked!

But suddenly there was a terrifying rumble beneath them and they all looked up in terror; the Zmei wasn't dead after all! It remained still for a moment before shooting towards them again with blinding speed, more enraged than ever. The Zmei's claws looked like a giant pair of scissors. The sharp talons gleamed in the sun and shimmered where they had been oiled to protect them from the elements. Mark and Lisa didn't stand a chance against its ferocious claws.

John managed to narrowly escape just in time - his eyes widening with horror as he witnessed his friends dying painfully at the hands of this merciless creature.

The mighty Zmei lurched forward, its massive claws snaking out towards John. But before it could snag the young man in its grasp, there was a thunderous clamor that shook the air - an army of warriors on horseback rushed in, swords held aloft and shining proudly under the midday sun. The boldness of these brave soldiers was awe-inspiring as they charged ahead towards the behemoth of a beast. Even with all their courage, none could suppress the fear that quivered through their veins at the sight of such a fearsome creature.

The battlefield was stained with blood, illuminated by the silver shimmer of swords clashing vigorously in a deadly battle. Arrows streaked through the darkness like blazing comets, aiming to pierce the Zmei with surgical precision. Steel and claws collided powerfully as the beast roared loud enough to shake the heavens. Blood curdled cries bellowed from both sides as each side fought for victory until eventually, the Zmei took its last breath and all fell silent.

Jon was in shock, filled with amazement and a strange sense of admiration as he watched this group of warriors fight fiercely for their freedom and to save his life. He could feel the pain in his body as he was dragged away by them - he had no idea who they were or how they had come to be there, but in that moment he knew he wanted to join forces with them. He saw their swords gleaming in the sun and felt an awe at the power that seemed to radiate from them, capable of defeating any creature that threatened them.

$$\Delta\Delta\Delta$$

Leshy

In Slavic Russia, The forest was lush and vibrant, with towering evergreens giving way to brightly colored deciduous trees. The treetops swayed in a breeze, sunlight dappling through their branches. Moss carpeted the ground and wildflowers bloomed in clusters around small streams and ponds.

The forest smelled sweet and earthy, with a hint of freshly turned soil, pine needles, and fallen leaves. The smell of fresh rain still lingered on the trees, along with fragrant flowers and fruits that grow amongst them. It was full of mysterious sounds - the whispering of the wind through the trees, the creaking of branches, the chirping of birds, and the occasional rustle of animals moving through the underbrush.

The whisper of the droplets, like a string quartet whispering in a cellar; the condensation, on the leaves, like a fine moist powder on stone with a hint of leather; the night, with its transparent and cold depth, like stale exhaustion, as if it were the night at the end of the world.

The Leshy, a forest spirit, was wandering through the trees. The Leshy was a tall and lanky figure, with eyes the color of emerald leaves and hair like golden autumn leaves. His skin was pale and luminous, with a faint shimmer that glowed in the sunlight. He wore a long green robe with intricate details embroidered into its fabric. His feet were bare but he moved gracefully, as if he were dancing among the trees. He carried with him the scents of nature – wildflowers, damp earth, lush foliage, and fragrant herbs. His presence was marked by a delicate aroma of sweet honey and spice. His movements were like a gentle rustle of wind through the trees, his voice a soft whisper that crackles like kindling as it echoes through the forest. He spoke with wisdom and humor, a deep reverberation that soothed and comforted the creatures of the forest.

The Leshy's days were filled with laughter and joy as he wandered through the forest, talking to its creatures. He had a playful spirit and enjoyed causing mischief - though never anything too malicious. His voice could be heard among the trees, playfully singing and whistling. But no matter how hard he tried, he couldn't escape from the ache in his heart - a longing that was ever-present and growing more intense. Even amongst the life of the forest, he felt more alone than ever before.

One day as he wandered through the forests, he came across a woman who was so beautiful that she took his breath away. Her skin was pale and luminous, glimmering in the sunlight. She wore a long green robe with intricate details embroidered into its fabric. Her eyes were the color of emeralds and her hair was wavy and cascading down her back in soft waves. Her presence was marked by an aura of beauty and grace that pierced through the forest like a ray of light.

But when she saw him, A low hiss slipped from her lips, echoing like a warning bell in the forest as her serpents slithered around her feet. Her voice was soft and gentle, like a murmuring whisper in the night, but when her emotions stirred it echoed with a strength that could rattle the trees.

Leshy's heart raced as he realized the truth. The figure before him was no mere mortal, but Medusa herself - the Gorgon of legend with a gaze that could turn flesh to stone. Yet still, he felt an unbearable pull towards her, unable to resist the tantalizing danger that lurked beneath her beauty. It was as if she were poison, and Leshy knew it would be his undoing. But even so, he found himself inching closer, desperate to get closer to her and feel the heat of her skin against his. The temptation was too much to bear, and Leshy surrendered himself to her seduction - knowing full well that it may very well lead to his downfall.

And so, they began to talk. Soft conversations in hushed voices that echoed through the night as they discovered shared passions and interests. They talked of history, love, nature and more - a delightful contrast between their wildest dreams and darkest fears. As time went on the air was filled with laughter - accompanied by playful banter that made Medusa blush with delight and Leshy's heart skip a beat every time her serpentine gaze met his own.

Soon enough it seemed like their destinies had finally aligned after centuries apart - each one finding another soul whose beauty mirrored theirs beyond words or measure could describe it all. As if an ancient mystery was being unraveled before them until there were no secrets left unheard; only truth remained unspoken between two hearts beating in perfect harmony from then onward.

As the days passed, they grew closer, sharing secrets and stories as they explored the forest together. They would lie in the grass, talking and laughing as they gazed up at the stars. They would dance around the trees, Medusa's serpents writhing in the air as they moved. One evening, as they were sitting by the fire, Leshy said to Medusa, "You know, when I first saw you, I was afraid. But now, I can't imagine my life without you." Medusa looked down, her snakes hissing softly. "I am a monster," she said. "No one can love me." "I love you," Leshy replied, taking her hand. "And I always will."

And so, they gave into their passion. They embraced each other, their bodies entwined as they kissed deeply. Medusa's snakes writhed in the air, hissing in ecstasy as she moaned softly.

In that moment, the two were no longer two separate beings - their hearts melted together as they kissed, creating a passion and joy unlike anything either of them had ever felt before. Their love was wild and beautiful; possessed with a fire that lit up the night sky in spectacular oranges and purples while mysterious songbirds filled the air with music. The stars twinkled brighter than ever above as Medusa's serpents entwined around Leshy - protecting him from any harm even whilst in her embrace.

And so it went on for days - passionate nights between friends who looked upon each other through lovers' eyes until one morning when both awoke to discover something magical: Nature itself seemed alive around them- trees rustling softly against one another like whispering secrets in a language neither of them could understand or decode but which stirred something deep within their souls nonetheless . It was almost like nature herself understood what profound beauty this union brought about into its world, strengthening both Mortals' bond even still through awe-inspiring wonderment every step of their journey thereafter!

Soon, many moons had passed and the two were wed in a beautiful ceremony that lasted for days. They settled down in Leshy's forest to raise a loving family - with three beautiful children now living among them. Each one was blessed with charmed hair, skin of porcelain white, and eyes shining like sapphires imbued with an inner flame burning endlessly! The eldest daughter held Medusa's wisdom while the middle child carried Leshy's wild spirit. But it was their youngest son who stole away their hearts completely; his mischievousness knew no bounds while his charm possessed him whenever he desired something or someone! For many years, they were happy. They roamed the forest together, free and wild, and they loved each other deeply.

Leshy and Medusa also made sure to pass on all the wisdom they'd learned over the years to their children, teaching them about how absolutely precious nature is. They taught them that each creature had a purpose in life, whether it be land or air-dwelling; even if angered by our actions or words we must learn humility and patience - for what goes around comes around! So when their daughter wanted to keep a pet snake from the forest as her companion, both Leshy and Medusa were adamant with watering down this desire of hers telling stories included lessons like why preying upon other creatures isn't respectful towards Nature itself.

The same was true for when one day she found two baby birds

abandoned on ground with no mother in sight - despite her crying face insisting otherwise both parents refused giving an excuse right away neither making light of nor letting go off explaining why tampering with another living being's destiny would not bring any good. Instead they provided innovative solutions such as creating makeshift nest using leaves while leaving food near where these babies first lay so that perhaps later one parent might surface looking out for its child again thus taking responsibility appropriately without parental interference!

They formed strong bonds between themselves ,their children but more importantly respecting Nature which remained prominent constantly guiding every decision made both inside home at bedtime sharing tales whilst simultaneously outdoors during walks across lush green meadows outlining ethics regarding flora & fauna alike.

One day, as the family was out on a walk, they stumbled upon a group of hunters, armed with guns and knives. The eldest daughter, with her knowledge of Medusa's wisdom, knew how dangerous these men could be to the forest and its inhabitants. She warned her parents, but they were not afraid. Leshy, with his wild and powerful spirit, stood tall and confronted the hunters, demanding to know why they were there.

The hunters sneered and mocked the family, calling them "freaks" and "monsters". But Leshy and Medusa stood firm, protecting their children and their home. With Leshy's strength and Medusa's cunning, they were able to drive away the hunters, leaving them with a warning to never return to their sacred land again.

After the confrontation, the family huddled together, grateful for their safety. But they knew that they could never let their guard down, for there will always be those who seek to harm nature and its protectors. They continued to pass on their wisdom to their children, teaching them the importance of standing up for what is right and protecting the delicate balance of the forest.

As the years passed, the children grew up to be strong and wise, just like their parents. They continued to roam the forest, free and wild, spreading the message of love and respect for nature to all who would listen. And though they faced many challenges along the way, they knew that they would always have each other, and the bonds that held them together would never falter.

As the years passed, Leshy and Medusa's love seemed to deepen even more. But as much as it had grown, so had their differences. As Leshy aged and his body weakened, Medusa remained young and strong. She could feel the chill of the coming winter, and knew that soon she would have to say goodbye. Tears streamed down her cheeks as she held his hands tightly in hers. "I will never forget you," she whispered, her voice full of both sorrow and love. "I will always love you." "And I love you too," he replied, his words barely audible. "I will always be with you, in the wind, the trees, and the stars." With those words, he slowly closed his eyes for the last time, leaving Medusa and her children alone in the forest.

Years went by, and the forest remained safe and untouched. Medusa wandered its paths alone, a lone guardian, for Leshy had long since gone. But in her heart, he was still there. His spirit filled her with strength and courage, allowing her to continue her duties as protector of the woods.

As time passed, Medusa's children grew to adulthood. And with their parents' guidance, they became guardians of the forest too. They roamed its paths and tended to its creatures, driven by a deep love and respect for nature.

But one day Medusa's time had come. Her snakes slowly left her body, leaving it cold and lifeless in the clearing where she had often shared moments with Leshy all those years ago. The family gathered around her to say their goodbyes one final time. And as they looked upon her face, free from the bonds of the serpents that had kept it hidden away for so long, they saw the face of true love - Leshy's love - etched into her skin forevermore.

And so it was that Medusa's earthly form found eternal rest in that same clearing she once called home with Leshy at her side; their bodies were entwined together just as their spirits had been throughout life: a testament to the power of true love between two creatures of the wilds.

ΔΔΔ

Banshee

The small town of Derry was a quaint and cozy place. The sun-drenched streets were lined with old-fashioned brick buildings, the windows glowing with warm yellow light. An old-fashioned clock tower stood tall at the center of the square, and beyond the cobbled streets and lush green fields lay the rolling hills of the countryside. On a pleasant night, the scent of freshly cut grass and flowers lingered in the air. There was also a hint of wood smoke from nearby fireplaces, and maybe even a whiff of freshly baked pies from one of the local bakeries.

It was cold there, and the rain fell like a blanket over everything, drowning the houses and drowning the streets and drowning the bags of trash that had once been people. People there were orange ice cream cones riding bicycles and writing books about martians who wore colors and sang songs. People there smelled like baloney sandwiches that had been covered in gasoline, and the sky was green and marbled and beautiful. Beyond the city was a vast, cold desert with a bright white light pulsing beneath it.

The locals had long whispered about a haunting wail that could be heard on the darkest of nights. The legend had it that the mournful cry was the harbinger of death, and that the creature responsible for it was the Banshee. The Banshee was a ghostly apparition with long white hair that flows like a river down her back. Her dress was a mix of soft, billowing fabric and dark, shimmering satin that clung to her figure like fog. Her eyes were pools of deep turquoise, and her skin is pale and almost luminous in the moonlight. The Banshee had no scent, as she was made entirely of spiritual energy. But those brave enough to get close enough could sense an aura of sadness and grief that seemed to surround her being. The Banshee's voice had an otherworldly quality to it, like a distant wind carrying whispers of secrets and sorrow. Her wail was mournful and haunting, a sound so piercing it can make one's blood run cold.

Enter Detective Connor, a caped crusader of justice who was determined to solve the mystery of the Banshee. He had heard of the legend and the eerie howls, and was not one to back down from a challenge.

Detective Connor stood tall and proud, draped in a black cape with a shiny silver badge clipped to the front. His eyes were a sharp and piercing blue that spoke of wisdom and courage. His face was stern but kind, and his hair was an unruly mop of brown curls. His body was lean and muscular, ready for any physical challenge that comes his way. Detective Connor had the distinct scent of leather and gunpowder, a reminder of the countless battles he had fought over the years. There was also a faint whiff of cigarette smoke, and an underlying hint of determination and courage that seemed to flow from him with every step he took.

Armed with his quick wit and trusty pistol, he set out to find the source of the haunting. The detective moved stealthily as he prowled the streets of Derry, his cape swishing through the air with each step. He clenched his jaw determinedly as he listened for any clues that may lead him to the source of the Banshee's wail.

The first few nights were uneventful, but on the third night, as he patrolled the streets, he heard the distinct sound of the Banshee's wail. The hairs on the back of his neck stood on end as he cautiously approached the alley where the sound was coming from. As he peered around the corner, he saw the Banshee hovering in the air, her long white hair and flowing dress billowing in the wind. She let out another mournful cry, and Connor braced himself for the worst.

"You shouldn't be here, detective," the Banshee spoke in a voice like a gentle whisper, "I am the harbinger of death, and you are meddling with forces beyond your control." Connor took a step forward, gun at the ready. "I'm not afraid of you, Banshee. Your reign of terror ends tonight."

The Banshee let out a bloodcurdling scream, and suddenly Connor was surrounded by a horde of ghostly apparitions. They clawed at him, pulling him down into the ground. But Connor was not one to go down without a fight. He fired his pistol at the ghosts, scattering them, and continued to charge at the Banshee. As the detective approached the Banshee, he noticed a subtle change in her demeanor. Her wails shifted from terrifying and menacing to sorrowful and mournful. Her figure seemed to sag, her shoulders drooping and her head bowed. Connor's grip on his weapon loosened as he took in the scene before him. An overwhelming sense of sadness seemed to come from deep within the Banshee. Connor felt it in his bones, a heavy sorrow that weighed upon him like a leaden cloak.

Like the angry growl of a wolf, the Banshee's cries began to sound hungry. It was a sound of nostalgic longing, the sort of long-denied hunger that tears the soul with its gnashing. The Banshee's wails grew insistent, pressing at his heart with their urgency. He looked at the Banshee's face. Her eyebrows were raised, her lips parted as if to close over her teeth. She looked hungry, and Connor wanted to help. He looked into her eyes and suddenly, he forgot everything else in the world.

Connor was startled when the Banshee spun around to face him, her eyes blazing with rage and tears streaming down her ghostly cheeks. "I cannot bear this any longer!" she screamed, "I am cursed to be the bringer of death; a fate I can never escape!" Her words resounded in his mind, stirring a sense of dread deep inside his soul, and he felt an overwhelming pity for the tortured creature before him.

Connor stepped away from the Banshee, his eyes scanning the dark forest surrounding them. "Is there any way to break the curse?" he asked pleadingly. The Banshee glanced down and shook her head sadly. "No, I'm afraid there's no cure for what I am," she replied in a whisper. Connor closed his eyes and took a deep breath, trying to search his mind for a solution. Suddenly, he had an idea. He opened his eyes, fierce determination burning in them. "What if you were to help me instead of hurt me? Together, we could make Derry a safer place where others could live free from fear."

The Banshee stared at him in shock. "What are you saying?" she asked. Connor sighed and replied, "I could use your help. You know things no one else does, and I'm willing to help you find a way to break the curse if you help me." The Banshee hesitated for a moment before nodding her head slowly. "Very well," she said reluctantly, "I'll help you. But only because I have no other choice."

Connor and the Banshee began their investigation into some of the strange events happening in Derry. They started by questioning locals and searching old records, but their leads kept going cold. It was growing more and more difficult to find answers, until one day they stumbled upon an old diary belonging to a woman named Sarah Blake.

Inside the diary were details of Sarah's dark past, including her involvement with a cult whose members were said to have mysterious powers. Connor and the Banshee realized that this cult could be responsible for the strange occurrences in Derry, and they decided to investigate further.

As Connor and the Banshee delved deeper into the mystery surrounding the cult, they also uncovered secrets about Sarah's own life. She had been cursed with a powerful magic that had doomed her to a life of sorrow and suffering. Realizing that the curse had been placed on her by members of this same cult, Connor suggested that if they could find a way to break it, then perhaps it would free them from whatever evil was at work in Derry as well.

They quickly set off in search of an answer. After days of searching through ancient books and speaking with mystics, they eventually discovered an ancient spell which promised to break any curse or hex with its power. With newfound hope, Connor and the Banshee cast the spell together, praying it would bring them peace at last.

To their amazement, the spell worked! In an instant, Sarah's dark magic was undone and she was no longer bound by its shackles. The Banshee too felt lighter than air as if she'd been freed from centuries of oppression.

Detective Connor and the Banshee formed an unexpected partnership, but their unique pairing was a match made in heaven. With his strength and her cunning mind, there was no criminal activity that could stand in their way. As they worked together, their growing bond of friendship enabled them to share their deepest secrets. Moved by her long-suffering plight, Connor swore he would not rest until he had uncovered the truth and found a way to free her from her ancient curse.

Connor had no idea what fate lay ahead of him. The Banshee was determined to escape her cruel curse, and she saw Connor as her ticket out. She had watched him over these months, observing his power and strength, believing his death could be the one thing that could set her free. But little did he know, the Banshee was ready to strike when the time was right, and she had something wicked in mind for poor Connor.

One night, as they patrolled the town, the Banshee suddenly turned on Connor. Her eyes glowed an eerie yellowish white, and her mouth opened wide to reveal a set of sharp teeth. He had never seen such a sinister smile from any human. A cold chill ran down his spine, and he raised his pistol to defend himself. But before he could react, she lashed out at him with long fingernails that were harder than steel. He tried to fight back, but she was too strong for him. She threw him across the ground like a rag doll. She overpowered him, pinning him to the ground with her long white hair. Connor struggled to break free, but it was no use.

The Banshee let out another scream, louder than before, and suddenly Connor felt his life force draining away. He gasped for air, trying to fight back, but it was no use. Within seconds, he was gone. Connor lay motionless on the ground, his life force drained away. The Banshee stood over him, feeling a strange mix of emotions. She had broken free from her endless cycle of torment, but she could not help but feel a sense of guilt for what she had done to Connor. In her heart, she knew she was responsible for his death and that she would have to live with the consequences of her actions.

She had betrayed the only friend she knew, and the guilt that weighed on her was tremendous. The cost of her actions seemed unbearably high, yet deep down she couldn't deny that something inside her had felt relieved in the moment. As she let out a sorrowful wail, it reverberated through the deserted streets of Derry.

From then on, nobody ever heard the Banshee's howl again; some said she moved to another town while others thought she had found peace. Some say she had left in search of forgiveness, while others thought she sought solace elsewhere. Either way, the Banshee's wail was never heard again. But no one will ever forget the tale of the Banshee and Detective Connor, and the unlikely friendship that ended in tragedy.

ΔΔΔ

La Ciguapa

The Hundred Acre Wood was a lush and beautiful forest filled with towering trees, lush green grass, and colorful flowers. The sun dappled through the branches of the trees, giving the forest a magical enchantment. Birds sang in the branches, and small animals darted from bush to bush. The air was crisp and clean, carrying the sweet scent of pine needles.

A winding path lead through the trees, past trickling streams and bubbling brooks. Wild brambles and thorny vines grew in abundance, creating a dense wall of green that surrounded the wood. The wood was home to an array of animals, some tame and some wild, but all living harmoniously together in this beautiful refuge.

The silence of the wood was broken by the sweet singing of birds, the rustling of small animals in the underbrush, and the distant sound of a waterfall. The breeze carried with it a gentle whisper that echoed through the trees, and as you wander deeper into the wood, it brought with it a feeling of awe and wonder.

Winnie the Pooh and his friends Tigger, Piglet, and Eeyore were on one of their usual adventures in the Hundred Acre Wood. Winnie the Pooh was a small, yellow bear with a red T-shirt and a big black nose. He had a kind, gentle face and a big juicy bottom. Tigger was tall and slender, with orange stripes, bright green eyes and boundless energy. Piglet was timid, with pink fur and big black eyes. Eeyore was gray with droopy ears and sad eyes.

As they walked, the group started to hear a strange chirping sound coming from further ahead in the wood. The sound seemed to be coming from a small cottage tucked away just off the path. Winnie the

Pooh's curiosity was piqued and he decided to investigate further. As they approached, they noticed that the cottage was surrounded by an overgrown garden filled with strange plants and flowers in every color of the rainbow. Some of these plants looked very exotic and unfamiliar, while others had a more familiar look. The front door of the cottage stood slightly open, as if inviting them inside.

What greeted them once they stepped through that door was something even more remarkable than what lay outside. The walls were lined with shelves filled with peculiar items and artifacts, many of which were totally unknown to Winnie the Pooh and his friends. There were jars full of glimmering gems, books filled with ancient stories and secrets written in languages none of them could understand, mysterious objects made out of metals and stones that seemed to twinkle in their own light, vials containing liquids both transparent and opaque – all sorts of strange things could be found here! The room itself felt alive – it seemed almost as if the objects on its shelves were whispering secrets about their past owners or how these things had come into being. It was an incredible experience for our adventurers as they explored this mysterious cottage deep within the Hundred Acre Wood.

Suddenly they stumbled upon a mysterious figure. The figure materialized out of the night with an almost supernatural speed. Her beauty was so otherworldly they were transfixed, as if seeing a vision of something beyond the realm of mortality. She seemed to behold some unknowable wisdom and her captivating eyes held them in a trance. There was something strange and mysterious about her that made them feel both enchanted and terrified. Her dark hair seemed to move like a shadow in the moonlight, clinging to her body as if it were alive. Her feet, strangely facing backwards, were hidden beneath her dress, but they seemed to vibrate with an otherworldly energy. Her face was pale and beautiful with deep, mysterious eyes that seemed to see right through you. She gave off a faint scent of jasmine and spice, almost like a subtle perfume that lingered in the air around her. As she came towards them, her footsteps were light and airy like a feather, barely making a sound as she moved.

"Who are you?" Pooh asked, curious but also a little scared. "I am La Ciguapa," she replied in a melodic voice that sent shivers down their spines. "And you have entered my domain." The friends were enchanted by her beauty and charm, and soon found themselves completely under her spell. It soon became clear that she knew more about this place than any of them ever could have imagined. As they ventured deeper into the woods, La Ciguapa told them stories of ancient gods and magical creatures, of forgotten secrets and lost civilizations. The stories were sometimes beautiful and other times disturbing, each one more captivating than the previous one.

The further they walked, the more unsettling things seemed to become. Strange shapes loomed in the shadows between trees as if they were watching them from afar. An eerie silence hung heavy in the air like a thick fog that seemed to be slowly suffocating their senses. The faint humming noise of some unknown creature seemed to follow them wherever they went; it was almost like something was trying to keep tabs on their movements or warn them from venturing too far into its domain. Despite their fear though, something compelled our adventurers forward – as if there was something unspoken drawing them closer towards an unknown fate somewhere deep within this enchanted forest.

The four friends trudged onward, their essences slowly eroding with every plodding step. Something grim and malevolent hung in the air like a thick oppressive fog, blanketing them in its oppressive gloom. Yet despite feeling increasingly fatigued, none of them made an effort to turn back. They were captivated by La Ciguapa's presence, powerless to deny her call no matter how uncertain they felt.

Suddenly, Eeyore pitched forward and crumpled into a heap of furry limbs. The others jumped in fright, as if waking from a deep sleep. For a few seconds there was silence as they looked around, reality finally dawning on them. Fear and dread filled their hearts as they realized that all along La Ciguapa had been luring them ever closer to a destiny more sinister than they could have imagined. They had ventured too far, too deep into the forbidden forest.

La Ciguapa turned, revealing a hulking beast with razor-sharp claws and fangs, its scales glinting in the moonlight. Its eyes were pitch-black and barren, its wings stretching out like an ancient bat's while its claws and fangs dripped with venomous saliva. The monster's scent was now a mix of putrid death and decay that clung to the air like a thick fog of dread. It carried hints of sulfur and smoke, a noxious mix of burning bile and hot tar. La Ciguapa roared, a monstrous cacophony of rasping hisses and growls. Its massive claws scraped and gouged the earth as it moved, its long tail swishing behind it with an eerie rustling sound. It exuded an aura of darkness that roared like a tempest. It reared up on four powerful legs and its powerful wings soared through the air like dark angels of death.

Tigger sprang into action, determined to save his friends from this terrifying beast. He fearlessly charged forward, ready to take on La Ciguapa himself. He bravely fought with all the strength and skill he had, dodging its powerful strikes and blocking any attack it threw at him. His agility and courage shone as he dodged its flaming breath and razor sharp claws. His battle cries echoed through the forest as he fought with a ferocity that was almost superhuman.

Unfortunately, Tigger was no match for La Ciguapa's power as his body soon succumbed to its relentless onslaught. His bravery lasted until the very end though; he had saved the rest of them from certain doom. As they watched in sorrowful silence, La Ciguapa for some reason retreated back into the shadows of the forest where it came from – leaving behind only a haunting echo of its roar that lingered long after it had gone...

The four friends mourned their brave friend, burying him in the dense foliage of the forest. They felt a deep sense of loss and regret for having ventured so recklessly into the forbidden forest. But they also felt grateful that he had given his life to save them and remembered him with fondness and reverence.

To honor their lost friend, they held a funeral ceremony for Tigger in the forest beneath a canopy of stars. The scent of wildflowers filled the air as the four friends sang solemn songs, recounting Tigger's adventures and courageous battles. They lit several candles to softly illuminate his final resting place, allowing his spirit to be embraced by the warmth of love one last time before departing this world forever. They vowed to be more careful when exploring the woods, and to always be on the lookout for danger.

As the group trudged along, a chill ran down their spines. Every glance around brought more fear and paranoia that something was about to happen. A whisper of wind rustled the leaves, followed by the crack of twigs underfoot as if someone—or something—was watching them from the shadows. Suddenly, they heard an eerie melody that reverberated through their souls. It was a ghostly voice, singing La Ciguapa's enchanting song. Instinctively they knew they had to flee, but it was too late—her glowing eyes filled with hunger appeared before them.

The friends desperately raced away, their legs trembling as they tried to put some distance between them and the evil creature that had already sapped so much of their strength. But despite their best efforts, they could feel her gaining on them. Every time they thought that they had escaped her clutches, she reappeared with a menacing darkness ready to consume them.

As La Ciguapa approached, Piglet let out a whimper before his tiny body trembled and hit the ground with a heavy thud. His small frame was motionless on the ground, eyes wide open and expression frozen in fear as if the life had been sucked out of him. The others cried out in despair as they realised what had happened. Realizing that Piglet was already dead, Eeyore and Winnie made a break for it while La Ciguapa remained fixated on the poor pig's corpse.

But La Ciguapa managed to grab Eeyore by the neck and pulled him upwards, her fingers clenching tighter and tighter as he twitched and struggled in her grip. His eyes bulged from their sockets, his mouth sputtered words of protest, before finally going limp and still.

Pooh's legs quaked with fear as the mesmerizing song of La Ciguapa played, drawing him closer and closer. He tried to resist but eventually succumbed to her power, tumbling to the ground like a ragdoll. She lunged forward with her sharp claws, ripping his body apart in an instant and consuming it hungrily, savoring every last morsel with delight.

The Hundred Acre Wood was now a place of sorrow and despair. The sky above was sullen and dark, filled with a thick fog that settled over the area like a heavy blanket. In the distance, the faint sounds of La Ciguapa's haunting songs could still be heard, an omen of what had happened to Pooh and his friends.

Rabbit and Owl were the first to arrive at the scene of horror. They were met with the reality of what had happened - Piglet's corpse lay still on the ground, Eeyore's head hung by a thread from La Ciguapa's claw, and Pooh's body was mashed up in a bloody pile nearby. Tears streamed down their faces as they mourned for their lost companions.

Meanwhile, Christopher Robin had been searching frantically for Pooh and his friends when he came across them in this state of devastation. He felt as if his heart would break in two as he realized how much pain his beloved friends had suffered. Stumbling over himself in grief, he stumbled back towards his house where he stayed locked away in his room for days on end until eventually emerging once more into the Hundred Acre Wood.

He gathered all of Pooh's remaining friends together and told them that there was still hope - that they could find another way to protect themselves from La Ciguapa before she could take any more innocent lives. He promised to help them find ways to stay safe from her presence whilst also carrying on with their adventures throughout The Hundred Acre Woods.

Days later, Rabbit led them back to where they had originally encountered La Ciguapa - armed with wooden spears crafted by Christopher Robin himself along with various other weapons provided by Owl who had gathered them from around The Hundred Acre Woods.

The atmosphere was thick with tension as they waited for La Ciguapa to make her arrival. The sky darkened and a chill wind blew through the trees - Their skins crawled with anticipation as they stood, not daring to move, eyes trained on the empty road ahead. La Ciguapa was coming, and whatever it brought with it, they could only guess...

ΔΔΔ

Ifrit

Millfield was a small, quaint town surrounded by rolling hills and lush green meadows. White picket fences lined the cobblestone streets, while scattered throughout are old fashioned lampposts and quaint shops. The town square hosted a bustling weekly farmers market with locals hawking their wares.

The air in Millfield was heavy with the smell of freshly cut grass and the scent of wildflowers carried on a gentle breeze. The nearby river added a subtle smell of wet earth and river moss, while the nearby bakery wafts the aroma of freshly baked bread throughout the streets.

The townsfolk could often be heard chatting away in their homes, or laughing in the streets while children played nearby. The church bells chimed to mark the hour, and birds chirped from the trees above. In the distance, there was a faint rumble of thunder as an approaching storm rolled in.

But the last few months were not regular in the small town of Millfield, strange things were happening. People were disappearing without a trace, and those who remained were plagued by strange dreams and visions. The usually peaceful streets of Millfield were cloaked in a foreboding darkness, as if a cloud of dread had descended upon it. People hurried through the streets, avoiding eye contact and looking over their shoulders in fear.

Alan, Jesse, Maya, and Lucas were best friends in high school. They shared an unbreakable bond and despite being unique individuals, they were always there for each other without question. Alan was tall and imposing with a broad chest and strong arms. Jesse was a bit shorter but was known for his wit and intelligence. Maya had olive skin and dark features, her confidence exuding with an inner strength. Lucas was the youngest of the group, with a mop of curly brown hair and bright eyes full of determination.

When they heard about the strange happenings in their hometown, the group decided to investigate and see if they could figure out what was causing all the chaos. After checking with local authorities and townspeople, they soon realised that no one had any idea what was going on. Determined to get to the bottom of it, the group started researching and looking for clues at places where people disappeared.

They combed through old records, investigated abandoned buildings, and looked for clues everywhere. They asked questions to those who still lingered around town, hoping that someone might know something. After weeks of searching and painstaking research, they finally stumbled across an ancient text which told a story of a powerful demon called Ifrit - an entity that could take human form and manipulate reality. Could this creature be responsible for these bizarre occurrences in Millfield? With not much else to go on, the group felt as if this was their only lead.

Guys, I think we're dealing with something really dangerous here," Maya said, her voice tinged with concern. "I know, but we can't just sit around and wait for it to come for us," Jesse replied. Lucas added, "We need to come up with a plan. We can't just go in there blindly and hope for the best." Alan, the group leader, nodded in agreement. "We need to figure out the Ifrit's weaknesses and vulnerabilities. We need to know what we're up against."

The group members worked in unison, scurrying around to gather weapons, maps, and other materials they deemed necessary for battle. Each person had an air of nervousness surrounding them, but even that fear didn't stop them from preparing for what was to come. They looked determined and ready to take on the challenge ahead of them. "Are you guys sure about this?" Maya asked, her hands shaking as she picked up the iron blade.

But the Ifrit was one step ahead and knew this group will be its last hurdle if it wanted to take over Millfield. The Ifrit followed each person in the group, its slithering, serpent-like movements easily distinguishable in the shadows. Its red eyes glowed in the dark as it attacked each person with its razor sharp claws, but for some reason it was unable to take a life, instead leaving deep gashes in its victims skin. It seemed to be playing with them, testing their strength and resilience, while growing stronger with each attack. The group members experienced a sense of dread as the Ifrit started showing up in their lives and was slowly and methodically stalking each one of them. When it did strike, it inflicted minor injuries, but seemed to be held back from killing its targets. There was a feeling of fear in the air, and the uncertainty of what this creature was capable of only made it more terrifying.

The group had no idea where the creature was coming from or when it would strike next, making them more cautious than before. Every night they would take turns patrolling their neighborhood, always on alert for any signs of the Ifrit's presence. During the day they worked together to devise a plan to defeat this powerful entity.

They researched every book they could find about the Ifrit, trying to figure out what kind of powers it possessed and how best to defend against it. After days of studying and strategizing, they finally managed to come up with a plan that just might work. With their nerves frayed but courage still strong, the four friends set out into the night in search of the demon that had been terrorizing Millfield. As they walked through the dark streets, not knowing what fate awaited them, a feeling of hope slowly began to wash over them - maybe this time things would turn out differently...

The mission was clear: lure the beast into an old, forgotten warehouse and use the mystic incantation to send it back to the netherworld. Adrenaline coursed through their veins like fire as they stood outside the creaky building, preparing for their darkest hour.

With a silent nod of acknowledgement, they crossed the threshold into what seemed like certain doom.

The air inside was heavy with tension, each step seeming to echo further and further into eternity. The shadows around them seemed alive, writhing in anticipation of the battle that was to come. As they reached out deeper into the depths of the warehouse, they could feel the presence that lurked within. It was time to face their foe head-on.

They gathered together at a crossroads made of crumbling concrete and weathered wood. Each held their respective weapons - talismans crafted with care; symbols of hope from ancient times - and cast their circle around them for protection against the malevolent force before them. With one voice, they began chanting a spell that had been passed down from generation to generation, invoking forces far beyond their comprehension.

The ritual had begun...and there would be no turning back now.

Jesse screamed with all her might. "We're in this together. We'll take the Ifrit down, no matter what." As they chanted the incantation, the Ifrit revealed its true form and attacked the group. Lucas and Jesse were the first to fall, their bodies flung back into the walls with such force that they were knocked unconscious. Maya and Alan tried desperately to keep the creature at bay, but it was too powerful. Its claws tore through the air like lightning, slashing them wherever it could reach.

Maya had just enough time to cast one last spell, which would help protect Alan from further harm. As she fell to the ground, her body lifeless and limp, only Alan remained standing in the face of certain death. He readied himself for a fight he may not survive and prepared for battle against an enemy far more powerful than anything he'd ever encountered before.

The Ifrit lunged forward again with a roar that shook even Alan's soul. With all his strength and courage, he fought back with every ounce of energy within him - swinging his talisman around in circles trying to ward off its attacks while reciting spells of protection under his breath. Alan was the last survivor left standing, his body trembling with fear as the Ifrit crept closer. "You are mine now," it spat, its voice menacing and cold. Alan knew he was in danger but fought back a wave of despair that threatened to overwhelm him. He had no choice but to face the unknown, no matter how uncertain the outcome. Alan felt panic rise in his chest as the Ifrit loomed closer and closer. He could feel its breath on his face, smell its evil presence, and hear its malicious laughter echoing in the abandoned warehouse.

In a last-ditch effort he heard a familiar voice inside his head - it was Maya's. "Alan, you can do this," she said with a conviction that gave him strength. With one determined thrust Alan plunged the iron blade deep into the demon's heart, destroying it for good. Everything around him began to shimmer and fade away until he found himself surrounded by an infinite blanket of darkness; a world unknown to him, yet strangely familiar.

"Maya? Jesse? Lucas?" he called out. But there was no answer. Alan found himself in a vast, desolate warehouse. The only light that illuminated the darkness was the faint moonlight through the broken windows. The walls were old and crumbling, and the air held an eerie stillness. He felt completely isolated, surrounded by a thick silence that seemed to swallow any sound he made. He felt a chill down his spine as he realized he was truly alone in this strange place. He looked around, but all he could see were endless rows of abandoned shelves and dimly lit corners. He was confused and afraid, uncertain if what had just happened was real or not. Had his friends been taken away? Was this all just part of a nightmare? He was filled with fear, feeling as if he had been transported to a place that was darker and more sinister than anything he had ever imagined.

The cold breeze brushed against Alan's neck, and he shivered. The Ifrit stared at him from across the room, its fiery eyes burning with hate. "Well done, human," it hissed. "You have destroyed my physical form, but my essence remains. And now, you will pay the price."

Before Alan could react, the Ifrit grabbed him and pulled him into a swirling vortex of smoke and flame. Alan was engulfed in a maelstrom of swirling smoke and intense flames. He felt himself being twirled and contorted as he was dragged through the unknown, his mind witnessing visions of unspeakable terror. The smoke spiraled around him like an impenetrable barrier, blocking out all light except for the faint glow of the distant moonlight. The flames gave off an eerie orange hue, illuminating the dark abyss that lay beyond.

Finally, the vortex spit him out into a dark, barren wasteland. Alan stumbled out into a desolate wasteland, with nothing but scorched earth and jagged rocks for miles. The sun seemed to have been obscured by a heavy black cloud, casting a deep shadow over the landscape. The air was thick with dust and the stench of sulfur filled his nostrils. In the distance, Alan could make out a faint red glow, like the horizon was alive with fire.

Alan's limbs felt like lead as he forced himself upright, his vision blurred and unsure. All around him was desolation, there were no signs of his comrades or a way out. The Ifrit's voice filled his head, "You are mine now, human. You will serve my desires for all eternity." But Alan wasn't ready to accept such a fate. He had to find a way to overcome the demon, no matter the consequences. He bared his teeth in defiance and spoke with a conviction that sent a chill through the air, "I will never bow to your whims, creature of the night!" A deep laughter emanated from the vacuum of space and Alan shivered at its sound. "We shall see about that, human," it said. "We shall certainly see..."

ΔΔΔ

Lilith

Vast as a blazing bonfire, Lilith had a body of coiling serpents dotted with eyes like the evening star. Lilith's dark form shifted in and out of the shadows, her purple eyes blazing with an unearthly light. Her skin was a deep ebony, her fingers tipped with long black claws. Her body moved like the wind, light and graceful, as if she was not bound by the laws of gravity. Lilith's presence was felt even before she was seen. An oppressive feeling hung in the air, a dread that seemed to be everywhere and nowhere at once. It was a low throbbing hum that reverberated in one's chest and head, almost like a distant roar that brought terror to all who heard it. Her voice was low and sibilant, like a creature of darkness that had been left unchecked for too long. It echoed in the shadows, sending shivers down the spine of anyone who heard it.

It was whispered amongst the villages that Lilith, a merciless demon of the night, terrorized newborns and pregnant women. No one dared utter her name out loud lest they incur her wrath. Babes were wrapped tightly in blankets and tucked away in their cradles, mothers clutched their unborn children within their bellies like they were valuable trinkets. Fearful eyes scoured every nook and cranny for shadows waiting to swallow them whole into darkness. No matter how hard people tried to protect themselves from Lilith, no barrier seemed able to contain her hatred. Every moment she screamed in the air for retribution, reverberating through the land with her ominous cries. Lilith was an evil witch that had been around since the dawn of time, a creature festering in malevolent power. Those that had crossed paths with her never escaped unscathed; it was rumored one look at her wicked countenance could rot a man's soul from the inside out.

Children would huddle together at night and tell campfire stories of a woman with red eyes and black wings that left only destruction in her wake. Her victims' families were wrought with grief all too familiar to those that had lost loved ones to this beast. For years, no one dared speak of what lurked in the night until a brave hero emerged from the shadows with a plan to vanquish Lilith once and for all. Yet unbeknownst to him, his fate was already sealed by his own ill-fated attempt; he'd soon become yet another victim of this ruthless demon.

In the small village on the edge of the vast forest, lived Sarah. Sarah was a young woman with petite features and wide, deep brown eyes. Her hair was a light chestnut color, pulled back into a tight braid that accentuated her narrow face. The faint aroma of lilacs lingered in the air around Sarah, along with the smell of freshly cut wood and baking bread from her humble homestead.

Sarah's husband, Jack, had gone away on a hunting trip just as the months of her pregnancy wore on. She was due any day now and the midwife hadn't been heard from yet. Sarah was determined to have this baby alone despite Jack being away and the midwife not arriving in time.

At first, Sarah thought she'd be able to cope alone but shortly after midnight her labor pains began and all thoughts of managing on her own dissipated. She wanted nothing more than for someone to help her through this ordeal - yet here she was, all alone with only fear and anxiety keeping her company. Her water broke soon after that and Sarah knew it wouldn't be long before she had a baby in her arms - whether she liked it or not.

The hours passed slowly as Sarah writhed in pain, wishing desperately for someone who could help relieve her suffering but no one came. As dawn broke, a steady rhythm of contractions filled the room like clockwork coming ever closer together with each passing moment until Sarah could barely catch her breath between them. All around her everything seemed to slow down; time seemed almost frozen except for the waves of pain that crashed over her body with relentless ferocity.

Then finally, when hope seemed lost and exhaustion had taken hold of Sarah's weary body, a sharp cry pierced through the silence; announcing the arrival of a new life into this world – it was a boy! After some effortful pushing and coaxing from his mother, he emerged into existence amidst an atmosphere of quiet elation and awe at what had been accomplished by such a fragile human being.

As Sarah held her newborn son in her trembling arms, a deep, ferocious growl reverberated through the room, causing her to shiver with fear. She slowly raised her eyes to see Lilith at the window, illuminated by an eerie, luminescent light that seemed to seep from her very soul. Her gaze was piercing and feral, full of hunger and malice.

Sarah held her newborn close to her chest. Fear rose in her heart as Lilith's shadow materialized from the darkness outside. She had heard tales of Lilith's power, and cursed herself for not believing them until now. With no time to spare, Sarah tried desperately to protect her precious bundle, but it was futile. Lilith's talons were as sharp as daggers, and with one swift motion she tore the baby from Sarah's arms. In a single moment, her son was gone forever into the night.

When Sarah's husband arrived home later that day, he found his wife broken and weeping, inconsolable in the face of such tragedy. He knew Lilith had taken their child when he saw the empty cradle in the corner. He pulled Sarah closer and together they mourned what had been lost; a piece of their souls had been torn away with their beloved son. The days and weeks that followed were filled with sorrow and despair. Nothing could ease Sarah's ache; her life felt so incomplete without her son.

Every evening she would stand at the edge of town, gazing out into the blackness for any sign of his return. But there was nothing, only emptiness. It seemed like a cruel joke that one who brought such immense joy into this world could be taken so suddenly without warning or mercy. And yet, despite it all, one thing remained unchanged: Sarah's love for her child was eternal, never waning nor fading even in death.

Years passed, and the village grew and prospered. But there were always whispers about Lilith, an evil demon who stole newborn babies and brought death to those undeserving. For years, they lived in fear of this creature, never daring to travel too far from home. Then one day, a stranger from the North arrived. He had broad shoulders and a stern face, his dark eyes seemed to look into your very soul. The townsfolk instantly recognized him for what he was - a hunter of demons and monsters. His name was Gabriel, and he had come to rid them of Lilith once and for all.

He moved through the town like some legendary hero of old, strong and fearless even against the unknown. Everywhere he went, the people watched him with curiosity and nervousness, hoping that he could fulfill his promise and protect them from harm.

Gabriel knew there would be no easy fight ahead; Lilith was cunning and powerful, her victims many and her victims young. But Gabriel came prepared - with weapons made from silver blessed by the church and magical talismans sewn into his clothing, he felt ready to do battle with the Demon Queen.

He ventured into the depths of the forest alone in search of Lilith's lair, determined to return victorious or not at all. For days he searched until finally he heard faint cries coming from deep within a cave hidden behind a dense wall of trees. Taking a breath for courage, Gabriel unsheathed his sword and stepped inside.

Time seemed to slow as darkness surrounded him and something cold touched his skin. There she was, Lilith herself - lurking in the shadows like a ghostly apparition. She was terrifying, her eyes blazing with an otherworldly fire, her talons sharp as knives. Gabriel knew that he had to act quickly. He drew his sword and charged forward, slashing at Lilith with all his might. But she was too quick, too elusive. Every time he struck, she was gone, disappearing into the shadows and reappearing just as quickly. The battle raged on for hours, until finally, Gabriel was able to land a decisive blow.

Lilith howled in pain, her form dissolving into a swirling vortex of darkness. And then, just as suddenly as she had appeared, she was gone. Gabriel emerged from the forest, battered and bruised, but alive. Back in town, news quickly spread about Gabriel's heroic deed; cheers rose up from every corner whilst children hung banners along the streets proclaiming his greatness. From that day on Gabriel was known throughout the land as the man who conquered evil and restored peace back to his people. But he knew that the memory of Lilith would stay with him forever, haunting his dreams and reminding him of the dark, terrifying world that lay just beyond the reach of human understanding.

Despite the triumph over Lilith, Gabriel knew that his work was not done. The deafening howl of her descent still rang in his ears, and he knew that there were countless other demons out there, waiting to strike at humanity.

Years went by, and Gabriel settled into a quiet life with his wife and newborn son. He had always thought that his success fighting monsters was measured in dead bodies, but now he realized it was about something else. Success can be found in the very act of living.

Gabriel had thought he'd escaped the darkness that had once consumed his life, but his fears were confirmed when a familiar growl filled the night air. He awoke in terror, and rushed to his son's room - only to find it empty. He frantically searched through the house for any sign of his wife or child, yet there was nothing to be found. The fear of evil that had been dormant within Gabriel reawakened as he realized he was once again face to face with the same demon from which he had run.

A deep rumble penetrated the still air, sending icy chills through

Gabriel's body. He knew that sound all too well - a sound emanating from beyond his wildest dreams and deepest fears. With trembling fingers he grasped his ancient sword and rushed outside, barely registering the freezing gust of wind that bit his skin.

There she stood, shrouded in darkness with blazing eyes - Lilith, the woman who had haunted him since that fateful day. Standing before her, Gabriel felt more scared than he had ever felt before. He raised his sword as if its dull metal could protect him, though he already knew it was useless against her unearthly power. His heart raced and his stomach churned as Lilith's penetrating gaze bore down upon him. The silence between them was terrifying.

The moonlight illuminated the castle grounds, where Gabriel and Lilith clashed ferociously. In her grasp, the cruel demon clutched his beloved wife and child. He bellowed in rage, his sword shining like a star in the night sky. His swings were wild, charged with every ounce of strength he possessed. But Lilith was too powerful, parrying each of his strikes with her wicked skills. The battle seemed to last an eternity, and it felt as if Gabriel's soul would be extinguished by its ferocity.

Suddenly, in a moment of respite, Gabriel saw a chance to strike. Lilith was distracted, overreaching for the youngling she held captive. Without hesitation, he lunged forward and thrust his blade deep into her heart with all his might. Lilith's wail echoed through the dark chamber and it was not one of agony or anguish. It was a feral snarl that reverberated with laughter, taunting him even as she looked like giving up her life. Her eyes filled with hatred for Gabriel, burning brighter than any fire ever could have.

She withdrew the sword from her heart with a sickening squelch, as if it were a mere splinter under her skin. And then she hurled it at Gabriel's cringing face, watching with satisfaction as he fell to his knees and gasped for breath. It was all too clear to him now that Lilith had become something beyond human, beyond demon, more powerful than he could ever hope to be.

Even as he struggled weakly against her grip on his soul, Gabriel glimpsed the horrifying scene unfolding before him. His wife and son, already half-dragged into the vortex of hell itself by Lilith's malevolent strength, writhed in agony and terror. He tried desperately to fight back, but it was all for naught; in the end, they were swallowed up completely, leaving only Lilith's hideous shrieks echoing through the void. The air grew still once more, leaving Gabriel alone with nothing but his own fear and despair. He knew then that there was nothing left for him in this world - not without his family to share it with. So he sank slowly to the ground, knowing that he would never find peace again.

Gabriel's screams ripped through the still night air, a cacophonous howl that tore at his throat. He voiced his anguish again and again, each ragged cry cutting into him as he let out wave after wave of pure terror. His face twisted in despair, contorted by agony and sorrow until it was barely recognizable. "Noooooooooooooooooooooooooooooooooooooooooooo...," he shrieked, the words reverberating across the landscape like a thousand echoes, draining him of every last ounce of energy. The silence that followed was crushing, Gabriel's voice wholly spent.

ΔΔΔ

Onryō

Detective Takeshi smelled of cigarettes, a hint of cologne, and sweat from a hard day's work. Tall and imposing, he was broad-shouldered, with a strong jawline and furrowed brows. His eyes were sharp and piercing, his suit impeccably tailored. His gait was confident and purposeful. He was just about to call it a night when he was summoned to a grisly scene of bloodshed in an ancient, decaying mansion on the outskirts of Tokyo. Though exhausted, he still spoke to the person on the phone with kindness. His voice was deep and authoritative as his words were spoken slowly and carefully, like each one had been thoughtfully decided.

The tires of his car screeched against the pavement as he raced towards the crime scene, and through the racing wind he caught glimpses of the cityscape; an endless sea of glass and steel stretching out beneath a smoggy sky. The outskirts of Tokyo were lined with old wooden buildings with falling roofs and shutters, small shrines and temples, narrow alleys that lead to secret places. Tall grasses that bend in the breeze, street lamps that flicker in the night, foliage that rustles in the wind. The air was filled with the scent of smoke and smog, a sharp, metallic smell that hangs in the air like a heavy blanket. The sound of distant traffic filled the air, punctuated by the occasional screeching of tires or honking of horns. The wind howled through the buildings and dust swirled through the streets.

Takeshi was determined to reach the crime scene with haste; whatever lay ahead of him, he would face it with steadfastness. He could almost feel the anticipation building within himself as he raced toward the destination, every step closer potentially bringing him closer to unearthing a horrific truth. The darkness of the night seemed to close in around him, and the fog brought a certain chill to his bones that unsettled him further. Despite his unease, Takeshi steeled himself and kept driving, pushing through the dense atmosphere until at last he reached his destination.

An eerie quiet engulfed the scene as Takeshi's car pulled up. The police officers who had greeted him were trembling with fear, refusing to take a single step inside the mansion. There was no doubt that this would be no ordinary case, but Takeshi was used to dealing with difficult challenges and wouldn't waiver in his pursuit of justice. He steeled himself as he stepped over the threshold and into the building. He was immediately overcome by an overwhelming feeling of dread as soon as he entered the mansion. It seemed like time had been frozen here, and even the air itself carried a heavy sense of history and tragedy. Nonetheless, Takeshi pushed on, determined to uncover whatever secrets lay hidden in the shadows of the past and bring those responsible for it to justice.

Takeshi's steps echoed miserably as he ventured through the empty mansion. Every corner that he turned, every door that he opened revealed yet another dreadful secret within. As though they were summoned by his presence, ghostly whispers and moans drifted in the air, hinting at something disastrous beyond the gate of the manor. The chill in Takeshi's bones intensified as he heard an otherworldly scream split through the silence. He ran towards it and soon arrived at its source. There, on the cold marble floor lay a woman with her throat cut open - too wide to be natural. Her neck was bent in half, reaching her stomach while her feet almost touched her head. Is she dead? He wondered before noticing her chest moving rapidly up and down. No, she is alive! He thought with horror as the woman whispered "Onryooooo!" in his ear. Her words lingered long after her breath had ceased forever.

The case was clearly beyond the scope of Takeshi's experience, and it weighed upon him heavily to arrive too late to save the victim. The culprit was long gone by the time Takeshi arrived, and he could only salvage a single clue - a crystal phial filled with a thick, yellow liquid, the words "Dismiss all hope" etched into its surface. The identity of the intoxicant would have to wait, and in any case, Takeshi had his own questions to answer. Why had the killer left such a note? And how could he arrest the culprit if nobody stayed alive to point a finger at him?

The next morning, Takeshi was back on duty, but his head was filled with questions that he couldn't answer. His usually stoic facade was replaced by a face of despair and frustration. He knew that the answers were within reach, he could almost smell them on the air, but it wasn't as if they had just fallen off a tree. He had to work hard to find them. He had to work hard to save more people. This was the fight of Takeshi's life, and he was ready to risk everything to find the truth.

Takeshi's investigation had led him to the seediest parts of the city where he met with a man or was it a woman, known as PD. They supplied high-end intoxicants to the rich and powerful of the city. Takeshi knew that he had to take a risk and talk to this person to find out what was in the phial he had found. In a dark alleyway, Takeshi waited for PD, his hand resting on his holster. It was only a matter of time before they arrived with an entourage of henchmen in tow.

Takeshi stood his ground and approached PD. "I need to know what was in the phial," Takeshi said sternly. PD smiled and said, "Why should I tell you?" Takeshi replied with a cold, hard stare. PD seemed to understand that she wasn't going to get away with their usual tactics, so PD sighed and said, "Fine, I'll tell you what you want to know. The phial contained a highly concentrated dose of Onryō poison." Takeshi's heart skipped a beat. Onryō poison was notorious for being untraceable and deadly. It was a poison that caused hallucinations of ghosts and spirits, and he knew that whoever had used it on the victim was skilled in the art of assassination. "Who would be capable of using such a poison?" Takeshi asked. PD chuckled and said, "You're asking the wrong person, Takeshi. But I can tell you this: whoever did this wanted to send a message. A message that says, 'You can't hide from me, I will find you no matter where you go.'"

Takeshi's mind raced with possible suspects, but he knew that he needed more information. "Thank you," he said before turning to leave. "Oh, and Takeshi," PD called out. "Be careful. The person who used that poison is dangerous. More dangerous than you can imagine." Takeshi nodded and left the alleyway, his mind filled with a newfound determination to catch the culprit.

As he delved deeper into the investigation, Takeshi soon found himself in the company of a woman named Akiko. She was a renowned assassin who had eluded capture for years, and Takeshi knew that if anyone could help him catch the killer, it was her. They met in a rundown tavern on the outskirts of the city, where Akiko listened intently to Takeshi's story. "So, you want me to help you catch this killer?" she asked. Takeshi nodded. "I know that your skills are unmatched, and I believe that together we can catch this person." Akiko smiled, her eyes glinting mischievously. "You're right, my skills are unmatched. But it won't come cheap." Takeshi knew that he would have to pay a high price for her services, but he was willing to do whatever it took to catch the killer. For the next few weeks, Takeshi and Akiko worked tirelessly to track down the killer. They followed leads, questioned suspects, and took risks that most wouldn't dare to take. As they got closer to the truth, they knew that danger was lurking around every corner.

One night, they found themselves in a dimly lit alleyway, the sound of their footsteps echoing off the walls. They had received a tip from an informant that the killer was going to be at this location, and they had come prepared. Takeshi silently unsheathed his sword and held it at the ready, while Akiko drew her two lethal daggers. They moved forward cautiously, their eyes scanning the area for any sign of movement.

Suddenly, a figure emerged from the shadows. It was a woman, holding a small vial in her hand. But Takeshi recognized her as PD he had spoken to weeks before.

PD's eyes widened in recognition as she saw the two assassins. "What are you doing here?" they spat. Takeshi stepped forward, his sword glinting in the moonlight. "We're here to catch the killer," he said, his voice cold and determined. PD snorted. "You'll never catch them. They're not human. They are something else. They are Onryo!" Takeshi tensed, ready to attack. But before he could make a move, PD raised their arm and flung the vial at them. It shattered on the ground, releasing a thick cloud of Onryō poison. Takeshi felt his head spin as the hallucinations began to take hold. He saw ghostly figures dancing around him, their laughter echoing in his ears. He stumbled forward, swinging his sword wildly at the apparitions.

Akiko grabbed his arm, pulling him away from the Poison Dealer. "We need to get out of here," she yelled. Takeshi nodded , his mind clouded with the effects of the poison. Together, they stumbled out of the alleyway and into the cool night air. As they walked unsteadily down the street, Takeshi could feel his body beginning to shake. Akiko's voice sounded muffled, as if she were speaking through a thick fog. He knew that they needed to find a way to counteract the poison before it was too late. "Where can we find an antidote?" Takeshi asked, his voice slurred. Akiko paused, her eyes scanning the dimly lit street. "There's a healer I know just a few blocks from here," she said. "But we need to hurry." With Akiko's help, Takeshi stumbled down the street towards the healer's shop. As they approached the door, Takeshi collapsed against the wall, his head spinning. Akiko pounded on the door, shouting for the healer to come out. Finally, the door swung open and an old woman emerged, her eyes sharp and piercing. "What's the matter?" she asked, her gaze taking in their disheveled appearance. "We've been poisoned," Akiko said, her voice urgent. "Can you help us?" The healer nodded and invited them inside. She mixed up a bitter-smelling potion and gave it to Takeshi and Akiko to drink. Takeshi could feel the effects of the poison beginning to subside, the ghostly images fading away. "Thank you," Takeshi said, his voice weak. The healer nodded. "You were lucky this time," she said. "You should be more careful."

Takeshi and Akiko thanked the healer and stumbled out of the shop, still feeling weak but relieved that the worst of the poison was over. As they made their way back to their hideout, Takeshi couldn't help but feel a sense of unease. PD had been a formidable opponent, but they were doing someone else's bidding and he knew that they couldn't let their guard down again. "We need to find a way to take her down," he muttered under his breath. Akiko nodded, her face set in determination. "We'll figure it out," she said. "But for now, we need to rest and recover." Takeshi nodded in agreement. They had narrowly escaped the PD's trap this time, but next time they might not be so lucky. As they arrived back at their hideout, Takeshi collapsed onto his bed, his mind racing with thoughts of revenge. He knew that he would stop at nothing to take down PD and Onyro and put an end to their deadly game once and for all.

The following days were filled with meticulous planning and reconnaissance as Takeshi and Akiko sought to learn everything about PD. PD was the The Poison Dealer, a notorious and elusive figure in their world, whose poison had killed countless people and left even more suffering from its effects. But Takeshi and Akiko wouldn't back down until they brought her to justice. Takeshi spent long hours poring over maps of the city, trying to identify potential locations where the Poison Dealer could be operating from. Akiko, on the other hand, was in charge of gathering intel about the Poison Dealer's clientele.

Through their efforts, they learned that the Poison Dealer had a network of informants who supplied her with rare and toxic ingredients for her poisons. They also discovered that she had a heavily guarded lab deep within the city's underground tunnels where she brewed her deadly concoctions. After days of preparation, Takeshi and Akiko assembled a small team of skilled fighters who were willing to help them take down the Poison Dealer. They carefully planned their assault, drawing up detailed blueprints of the underground tunnels and assigning each member a specific role.

On the night of the attack, Takeshi's heart was pounding in his chest as they descended deeper into the tunnels. With each step, he knew that they were getting closer to their ultimate goal - taking down the Poison Dealer. As they neared the entrance to the lab, they were ambushed by the Poison Dealer's henchmen. A fierce battle ensued as Takeshi and his team fought valiantly against their attackers. Finally, they were able to break through their defenses and burst into the lab. The Poison Dealer was standing in the center of the room, calm and collected despite the chaos around them. Takeshi could feel his blood boiling as he confronted D. "You've caused so much pain and suffering with your poisons," he spat. "It's time for you to pay for your crimes." The Poison Dealer simply smirked, unfazed by his anger. "You think you can take me down? You're just a bunch of amateurs compared to the power of my poisons. I have the backing of the Onyro!"

With a flick of her wrist, she uncorked a small vial and tossed it at Takeshi's feet. A cloud of noxious gas erupted from the vial, causing Takeshi to cough and wheeze as he struggled to breathe. His eyesight began to blur, and he felt himself losing consciousness. Akiko rushed to his side and administered an antidote that she had prepared beforehand, saving his life. The rest of their team continued to fight against the Poison Dealer's henchmen, but the Posion Dealer had vanished in the chaos. Takeshi knew that they had failed this time, but he was determined not to give up until they brought the Poison Dealer to justice. As they retreated back to their hideout, Takeshi swore that he would succeed in their mission, no matter what it took.

Despite the setback, Takeshi and his team persisted with their mission to end the Poison Dealer's reign of terror. They spent weeks gathering intel and planning their next move, determined to not let their previous failure dampen their spirits. Takeshi, however, was plagued by nightmares of Onyro. No matter how hard he tried to push those memories away, they kept creeping back into his thoughts.

One day, as Takeshi was training in the dojo, he saw Onyro standing in the corner of the room. Takeshi shook his head, knowing that it was just a hallucination brought on by his guilt and past trauma. But the figure continued to taunt him, urging him to give up on his mission and join forces with the dark side. Takeshi's nerves had reached their limit, and he grabbed the kitchen knife from its place on the counter. He felt a primal rage course through his veins. Quicker than thought, Takeshi drove the blade into Onyro's chest, only to realize in the next moment that it was Akiko that he had just killed. The life left her eyes as they met his in one last gaze, then her limp body slid down to the floor.

Takeshi was overcome with guilt and rage. He had just killed his most trusted partner. He vowed to never let such a tragedy happen again, and he set out on a suicide mission to take down the Poison Dealer once and for all. He gathered his closest allies and made a plan: they would sneak into their lab during the night, when she was least expecting it. Armed to the teeth, they charged into battle against her henchman, determined to finally bring justice to their fallen comrade. The fight was brutal but short-lived; Takeshi's team managed to overpower the Poison Dealer's forces and corner her in their own laboratory. Knowing that he had no chance of survival if he stayed any longer, Takeshi ran towards the Poison Dealer with one last burst of energy. Taking out his homemade bomb, he shouted "This is for Akiko!" as he hurled himself at her along with it. The explosion rocked through the lab, turning it into ashes within minutes. In that moment of ultimate sacrifice, Takeshi succeeded in bringing an end to the Poison Dealer's reign of terror - though at great cost to himself. As his body lay amidst the ruins of destruction, his soul filled with peace knowing that justice had been served and that Akiko could finally rest in peace.

$$\Delta\Delta\Delta$$

Big-Foot

Tom slammed his beer can on the bar of The Stumble Inn with a loud thud, his eyes wide and wild. "I'm telling you, Jake," he exclaimed, spittle flying from his lips. "It was huge, had fur all over its body... and it was walking upright! Like a man!"

Jake sighed and rolled his eyes. "You've been drinking too much tonight, Tom," he said. "Look, I believe you—but you probably just saw some animal. A bear or something." "No way! It wasn't like any bear I've ever seen before," Tom replied insistently.

The conversation had caught the attention of a few other patrons in the dimly lit bar. One of them cleared their throat and spoke up. "What did this thing look like?" Tom opened his mouth to reply, then paused for a moment as if carefully considering how to explain what he'd seen. Finally, he began again in a low, almost reverential tone. "It was big... about eight feet tall. Its skin was thick and dark brown—almost black—like it was wearing some kind of armor plating. And its eyes... they burned with an unholy light that scared me to my very core." The room fell silent as everyone at the bar stared slack-jawed at Tom's description. Even Jake seemed temporarily breathless with shock. Finally, one of the other patrons spoke again. "That sounds like something out of a nightmare! Did it do anything else?"

Tom shook his head slowly and took another swig of beer before responding. "No... it just stood there looking at me. That's when I ran away." Everyone went quiet again while mulling over what Tom had said, then finally one of them spoke up. "Sounds like Bigfoot to me."

Tom felt a chill, his eyes widening in disbelief as the man replied. "Bigfoot? Do you really believe that?" The man shrugged, scratching at his thick beard. "I don't know what to think. But there have been plenty of sightings around these woods for years."

Jake scoffed and chuckled, shaking his head. "You two are crazy. There's no such thing as Bigfoot." The old woodsman drew in on himself then, as if he was pulling a great secret into himself like an oyster tucking its pearl away from danger. His voice lowered, barely audible above the chirping of crickets in the background. "That may be true," he rasped. "But I've heard the howls myself late at night, deep in the heart of these woods. It's not any normal animal, not something I can explain away with science or reason." Tom felt a shudder run down his spine as he glanced uneasily around them, half-expecting something huge and furry to come crashing out from between the trees. He could almost feel some unseen presence watching him from the shadows, and he found himself wishing fervently that they were somewhere else, anywhere but here beneath this oppressive canopy of ancient pines. "Well," Jake said slowly, glancing nervously over his shoulder. "Whatever it is out here, let's hope it stays there."

Tom couldn't get the image of the beast out of his mind. He was determined to prove its existence, and so the following day he returned to the woods. Making his way through thickets and brambles, Tom heard a strange rustling sound that seemed to be coming from nearby. A chill ran down his spine as he slowly crept closer, expecting to come face to face with some unimaginable horror any second now. But instead, what he saw left him stunned: standing in front of him was not one creature but two. They were just like the one he had seen yesterday except bigger, their fur a deep red color instead of brown. Tom could hardly believe his eyes – all at once doubt and fear gave way to awe, as he realized that this was proof enough that there really was something extraordinary living in these woods.

The creatures were covered in shaggy dark red fur, with long arms reaching down to its massive feet, which seemed to be made of solid stone. One of the creature's head was large and round, with two piercing eyes that stared at Tom with a strange intensity. Its body seemed to shimmer in the sunlight, as if it were made of something otherworldly.

The air around Tom seemed to still as he watched the creature, his jaw dropped in disbelief. 'Bigfoot,' he breathed, barely able to get the word out of his throat. The creature slowly moved its head towards Tom, and their gazes locked for an eternity, or so it felt like it. His eyes felt like they were being pulled into the creatures black pits of bottomless night, the terror making time stand still. Suddenly, the atmosphere changed, and just as quickly as it had appeared the creature was gone; vanished back into the woods. Tom stood there rooted to the spot, a sense of awe washing over him. A chill ran down his spine as he realized what he had seen.

Tom staggered into the dimly lit bar, his head spinning. A cold sweat rolled down his face as he frantically looked around. He turned to Jake, eyes wide with terror. "I saw it again. Bigfoot!" he croaked out in a whisper, barely able to contain himself. Jake gave him an appraising look and sighed heavily. "Come on Tom," he said. "It's late and you've had too much to drink." But Tom knew what he had seen and wasn't about to be dissuaded so easily; he staggered closer to Jake and grabbed him by the arm. "No! I'm not crazy, I swear! I saw it clear as day just now - a huge creature, like nothing I've ever seen before!" His voice started to rise and his grip tightened on Jake's arm. "It was big and hairy, with glowing yellow eyes!" Jake pushed him away, trying to keep the peace in this dive bar full of drinkers at this late hour. "Alright, calm down," he said sternly. "Let me get you some more beer and maybe then you'll start making sense." Tom slumped into a nearby chair, still trembling from his experience, but knew that there was no way anyone was going to believe him; after all, who would ever believe something so outlandish? He sat there silently for the rest of the night, wondering if he'd ever lay eyes on Bigfoot again.

Tom's story of seeing a mysterious creature in the forest had generated quite a buzz around town. While some people laughed off his claims, others hung onto every word in anticipation that it could be true. He was determined to prove the validity of his sighting, but he wasn't sure if anyone would believe him.

He gathered a sinister crew of adventurers, each one with their own deadly set of talents. With malignant intentions they ventured out on their mission, like a hoard of fierce predators seeking out their prey.

There was Sarah, a sexy and skilled tracker with a keen eye for spotting clues in the wilderness. She had a lithe physique with curves in all the right places and her eyes scanned the terrain with focused intensity. Her long hair was made up of shades of brown and her skin was tanned from the sun. Clothing-wise she preferred to dress for both style and functionality, often choosing a combination of leather and denim.

Then there was Mark, an experienced hunter with a reputation for his accuracy with a rifle. Mark's frame was tall and muscular, his arms muscled from years of shooting. He wore a camouflage hunting jacket with multiple pockets filled with ammunition and survival gear. His face was rugged, with a strong jawline and piercing blue eyes. Mark smelled like manly cologne mixed with the forest's own natural aroma of dirt and wood smoke. He carried the scent of gunpowder from his rifle and the sweet smell of freshly mowed grass. The clink of a loaded chamber, the silence of a steady breath, and the thunderous crack of a well-placed shot.

And finally, there was Max, a seasoned outdoorsman who had spent years surviving in the wilderness. Max's figure was stocky and strong, his skin bronzed from long hours in the sun and his hair cropped short and easy. He wore comfortable clothing made for battling unforgiving wilderness, patches of leather stitched together for protection and multiple pockets filled with tools and supplies. His face was craggy and battle-worn, a facial map of scars from years of exploration.

Wrapped in the cover of night, the team marched on. With only a faint light from their flashlights cutting through the dense foliage, each step was made cautiously. Small critters scurried away with every rustle of leaves and branches. All hope seemed lost until they heard a distant call echoing from the depth of the woods.

Their hearts raced as the cacophony grew louder. Although fear had taken root in their souls, none dared move an inch away from the path Tom had left behind. Every so often, the sounds of twigs snapping echoed between the trees. As if almost in response to this noise, a low growl came out from within the darkness.

The team stopped in their tracks as goosebumps rose up on their skin. The ensuing silence was broken by another guttural roar that sent a chill up their spines and confirmed what they had come here for—Bigfoot was near. The team huddled closer together and braced for what would come next; but instead of charging ahead, they stayed there motionless, waiting patiently for the beast to reveal itself.

After a lengthy period of hesitation, they finally began to advance deeper into the forest, the air seemed to thicken with a sense of dread. With each crunch of leaves underfoot or rustle in the bushes, they felt chills ripple down their backs and icy shivers ran along their skin. They knew they'd crossed into another realm, one that could belong to a fearsome beast that may not welcome visitors. The hairs on the back of their necks stood at attention, sensing something was amiss. All eyes scanned widely to take everything in. Branches swayed gently as if influenced by an unseen hand. Steady creaks from tree limbs warned them to stay alert and aware of where they were going.

As the sun began to set beyond the river, Sarah stood in the middle of a circle, the fire burning in front of her. The flames danced and flitted into the sky, and she pulled a blanket around herself for warmth. Tom had walked down to the river, and his shoes crunched across the rocks as he neared the bank. Next to his feet were large tracks. She knew this was no animal; there was a toe pattern in the dirt that indicated it had five toes. "Do you see this?" Tom said. "We found them."

As the dark night began to enshroud them, they settled in for sleep. Tom and Sarah had been flirting with each other throughout the night, the chemistry between them that seemed to be bubbling beneath the surface just waiting for a chance to overflow. Beneath the blanket of the night, a fire had been ignited between them, one that could not be quenched by the passing of time.

Tom made his move, his hands exploring every inch of Sarah's body, caressing her soft flesh as he kissed her neck. The hunger manifested into something tangible as they ripped each other's clothes off. His mouth moved its way down to her ample breasts, suckling on them hungrily as she moaned in pleasure. Their love swirled like a kaleidoscope of color in their hearts; they were intertwined like two dancers closing out an exquisite ballet performance. His hands moved from her hips up to her chest, kneading her flesh until Sarah felt as if she was melting into his touch. After what seemed like hours of intense exploration, it all culminated with an explosive, soul-stirring climax that left them both feeling spent and satisfied.

The following day, the team stalked the trail of footprints, a desperate hunt inching them closer to their prize. With each step they felt the intensity of the situation grow, until it seemed like the air itself was humming with dread and anticipation. They knew they were entering hostile territory, one where any misstep could be their last. Fear coursed through their veins as they moved forward, ever closer to whatever it was they sought.

They found themselves in a remote part of the forest, far from any human settlements. As they approached a clearing, they spotted a family of Bigfoots - a majestic sight. Each creature was at least seven feet tall, with thick fur coats that glittered in the sunlight like a rainbow of colors. The rustling of the grass and leaves in the wind created a soothing background for the gentle grunts and high-pitched squeals of the Bigfoots. Each sound carried a note of contentment, making it clear that this family was at peace and unafraid.

Tom stood in shock as he watched the majestic creatures before him. He felt a wave of emotion wash over him - he had been transfixed by their presence ever since his first encounter with Bigfoot, and he realised they had never posed a threat to anyone. But as Tom's heart softened at the sighting, Mark saw a chance for glory. His ambition was searing, and with it came an intense inner conflict. He raised his rifle higher, ready to fire at any moment. Tom looked on in terror - he wasn't sure who was more dangerous now, Mark or the gentle giants that roamed before them. He knew that if they fired upon these peaceful beings, the world would be robbed of something special; something sacred. He had to act fast but without agitating Mark further. Tom spoke softly, forming words that were meant to soothe rather than alarm. "Mark," he said cautiously, "We are here for observation only - no-one has to get hurt".

"Stop!" Tom shouted, stepping in front of Mark. "We can't harm them. They're just living their lives peacefully."

Mark was determined, and his finger found the trigger before Tom could even react. The explosion of sound shattered the stillness, followed by a howling roar from one of the Bigfoots. Panic ensued as the other creatures rushed to defend their injured family member.

Tom screamed for everyone to back off, but it was already too late. He had awoken a sleeping giant, and the team found themselves in the midst of an all-out war. The Bigfoots were relentless in their attacks, strong and agile as they defended their kin. Firecrackers of terror filled the air as they fought with a vengeance.

Mark, Max and Sarah were each ripped apart by the hulking beast's that had descended from the woods. Tom could only look on in horror as his teams' lives were cut short. He tried desperately to help them, but it was too late; the creature had already dispatched its victims. The sight of Sarah's mutilated body, her breasts torn from her chest, would haunt his dreams forevermore. Tom barely managed to escape with his life, though not unscathed; he felt a sharp pain where his left hand should have been, and he realized that the monster had severed it in their struggle. With one last glance at his doomed comrades, Tom ran until exhaustion finally caught up with him. He collapsed into a heap in the dirt and wept until morning light rose over the smoldering ruins of what was once a beautiful forest.

Tom stepped into the Stumble Inn with a heavy heart, the memories of what had happened there years ago flooding back. He glanced around, his gaze finally settling on Jake. With a sad sigh, he said, "I told you that day that there was something out there in those woods, but you didn't believe me." "You were right, Tom," Jake replied quietly. "But even then I never thought it would come to this. I wish we had left Bigfoot alone; let them keep their secrets and live in peace." Tom nodded sadly, knowing that he had set in motion events that could not be undone. He stayed silent from then on, never telling anyone else about the magical creatures in the woods.

$$\Delta\Delta\Delta$$

El Hombre Del Saco

Snowflakes gently floated through the darkness. There was a stillness to the night—no lights to be seen, no people to be found. Everything seemed to be at peace, a perfect backdrop for Santa's task ahead. The scent of cold wintery air hung in the air; a hint of pine from the nearby trees mingled with woodsmoke from the chimneys. Silence. An eerie quiet was all that could be heard, save for the occasional sound of a distant car or barking dog. The air in Madrid was usually filled with the scent of freshly baked bread, wafting from the local bakeries. But on this night, there was nothing but a stagnant quietness to the city. Whereas normally one could hear people and traffic, now there was an eerie hush that seemed to nearly swallow the sound of a distant car or barking dog. The streets were empty and still; normally, vibrant buildings and active streets were blanketed in a soft darkness. Even the faint glow of the street lamps seemed to dim, as if they had been snuffed out by the stillness of the night.

As Santa flew through the air, he whistled a jolly tune that filled the night with a relaxing melody. His laugh was cheerful and hearty, a deep baritone that filled the air and spread cheer to all who hear it. Santa Claus smelled of freshly baked cookies and milk, and pine needles from the evergreen trees of his home in the North Pole. Santa had a rosy red complexion, bright cheerful eyes, and a white beard that reached his waist. He wore a bright red suit trimmed with white fur that contrasted against the wintery darkness around him. His large sack of presents was carried behind him, bulging with toys and goodies for all the good children of the world.

As he soared above the sprawling expanse of Madrid, a deep and sinister cackle ripped through the air, sending a chill through his entire body. The bone-chilling laughter seemed to linger and reverberate in his mind, threatening to swallow him whole if he dared stay a moment longer.

His head was a shapeless nest of shadows and coal, and he had no eyes that could be seen. His mouth was dark and cavernous and framed with cloak of ragged flesh. He was a hulking monster clad in skull and shadow and broken by the void. It's laughter was chilling. It was a throaty cackle that echoed through the night, threatening to drive away any who came close to him. He was a tall, dark figure shrouded in a long black cloak. A large sack was slung over his shoulder, bulging with the victims of his cruel traps. His hands were like talons, reaching out with long nails to grab a child's unsuspecting soul. A noxious and nauseating smell followed him, as if he had just crawled out of the grave. It's a mix of death and decay, like rotting flesh and burning sulfur. His touch was cold and slippery, like ice on your skin.

The children called him El Hombre Del Saco - the man in the sack - and they knew it was best to run when they saw him coming. His sinister silhouette sent chills of terror through the locals who whispered stories about El Hombre Del Saco, the dreaded child abductor who sought out unsuspecting young victims.

Santa Claus felt a chill run up his spine as he heard the sound of mocking laughter, echoing through the night air. He shook it off and tried to focus on fulfilling his task of delivering presents, but something was still off; he could have sworn he was being watched. He glanced cautiously around the room and peered into the shadows, only to find himself face-to-face with El Hombre Del Saco - the infamous Boogeyman. A deep dread filled Santa's heart and he stumbled backwards in surprise, but before he had time to react a bony hand grabbed him firmly by the arm. The Boogeyman stared at him with piercing black eyes, radiating suppressed rage.

El Hombre del Saco stared at Santa with a smirk of malicious glee.

"You should be ashamed of yourself," he intoned in a deep, resonating voice that seemed to shake the very walls around them. His words cut through the peaceful stillness like a dagger, reverberating through the air and driving home their meaning. Santa had been visiting children all over the world for decades—but unbeknownst to him, El Hombre del Saco was claiming some of them as his own. The revelation made Santa feel small and weak, its icy tendrils wrapping around his heart like a vice. He could not find the words to respond, and so he simply stood there in silence as El Hombre del Saco's grin widened even more.

Santa thrashed and struggled against El Hombre del Saco, but his efforts were futile as the villain's vice-like grip tightened around his body. With a malicious smirk, El Hombre del Saco shoved Santa through the door of the nearest house and slammed it shut behind them, trapping Santa in his grasp.

As Santa struggled to break free, he felt a sudden jolt of energy course through his veins. He closed his eyes and concentrated with all his might, drawing upon the magical powers that had served him so well throughout his career. With a burst of intense energy, Santa broke free from El Hombre del Saco's grip and stood tall, his eyes blazing with a newfound strength.

He looked around the room, surveying the horrors that El Hombre del Saco had inflicted upon the children. The walls were covered in blood, and the screams of children echoed through the halls. Santa felt a wave of anger and determination wash over him. He knew that he had to put an end to El Hombre del Saco's reign of terror once and for all. Santa closed his eyes and focused his energy, calling upon the magic of the North Pole to aid him in his fight. He felt the power coursing through his veins, energizing him and filling him with a fierce determination.

With a mighty roar, Santa charged at El Hombre del Saco, his fists raised high. El Hombre del Saco tried to dodge Santa's attack, but he was too slow. Santa's fists crashed into his face with a loud thud, sending the villain reeling backwards, blood spurting from his nose. Santa pressed the advantage, unleashing a series of punches and kicks that left El Hombre del Saco gasping for breath. Despite his injuries, El Hombre del Saco refused to go down without a fight. He lunged at Santa, his claws extended, and the two grappled fiercely, their bodies slamming against the walls and furniture of the house. The sound of shattering glass and cracking wood echoed throughout the room as they fought. The children who had been hiding in terror watched in awe as Santa and El Hombre del Saco battled it out. Even the Boogeyman had to admit that he had never faced an opponent as formidable as Santa Claus before.

But he was not one to give up easily, and he continued to fight with all his might, his claws tearing at Santa's flesh. Blood dripped from Santa's wounds, but he refused to give up. With a final burst of energy, Santa summoned all the magic he could muster and unleashed a powerful blast of energy that sent El Hombre Del Saco flying across the room and crashing through the wall. The Boogeyman lay motionless on the ground, defeated.

Santa breathed heavily, his body battered and bruised, but he had won. He looked around the room at the terrified children, and knew that he had to do something to help them. With a wave of his hand, he healed their wounds and wiped away their tears, filling them with hope and joy once more. He gathered them all in his arms and lifted them up, carrying them out of the house and into the cool, refreshing night air. The children shouted and cheered as they flew through the air, holding on tightly to Santa's coat and laughing with joy and excitement. As they flew over the city streets, Santa knew that he still had a lot of work to do. He had defeated El Hombre del Saco, but there were still many children out there who needed his help. He made a vow to never give up on his mission to bring peace and happiness to all children, no matter where they were.

But as they were flying away, El Hombre wasn't dead. Suddenly, he appeared in the sky, wings spread wide and eyes blazing with rage. With a terrifying shriek, he dived towards Santa and the children. Santa moved forward instinctively to protect the children but it was too late. El Hombre slashed at their heads with his razor-sharp claws and filled them into a large sack. He cackled maniacally as he soared through the air, intent on bringing further terror to children everywhere.

Santa was filled with rage and sorrow that these innocent children had been put in danger once again by this evil villain. He focused his energy, calling upon the power of Christmas Magic that coursed through him like a river of light. His fists blazed with a brilliant white light and he charged forward, determined to save these poor kids from this nightmarish monster once more.

El Hombre del Saco had expected an easy victory against this old man, but instead found himself facing an adversary worthy of his power. The two enemies clashed in mid-air as Santa launched an attack using all of the strength he could muster against El Hombre's dark magic powers. The fight raged on for what seemed like hours until finally Santa managed to land a devastating hit that sent El Hombre spiraling out of control towards the ground below where he crashed into a pile of snow and lay motionless amidst broken tree branches and shattered rocks . Santa quickly rushed down towards him but when he reached him there was no sign of life.

Santa looked back up towards the sky, relieved that El Hombre was no longer a threat to the children of the world. But as he did so, he noticed something moving out of the corner of his eye. He turned and was shocked to find El Hombre slowly getting up from the snow, his eyes flashing with renewed strength and determination.

It seemed that even with all of Santa's power, El Hombre was not dead after all. Santa took a deep breath and clenched his fists in preparation for another battle against this relentless enemy but El Hombre Del Saco was finally too fast for him. The villain sprinted towards Santa, each footfall reverberating off the icy walls of the alleyway. His hands were balled into fists and clenching something sharp in his grasp. The blade pierced through Santa's chest, and he dropped to his knees in agony. A thin stream of blood ran down his white coat as he gasped for air, his breaths came in shallow gasps as life ebbed away and he finally crumpled to the ground.

El Hombre Del Saco cackled with sadistic glee as he ripped Santa's head from his shoulders with brute strength. His hands quivered in delight as he shoved the severed head into the deep abyss of the sack and tightened the drawstring with a sickening snap.

"Merry Christmas, Santa," he said with a sinister smile. "And a happy new year to all my little friends."

ΔΔΔ

La Madre De Agua

Her form was imposing and regal, her eyes burning with righteous fury. She was said to shimmer with an emerald light, her body adorned with crowns of seashells and seaweed draped across her shoulders. The air around her carried the scent of salt, sea-spray and ocean algae. Her presence was like an invisible force bearing down on those nearby, making them feel suffocated and vulnerable. Her presence was accompanied by the sound of crashing waves, her echoing voice ringing through the air like a foghorn, demanding attention. The gusts of wind that whipped around her form tussled with the thunderous sound of her footsteps, as if she was walking on a wave of her own power.

She was said to have a hide of solid obsidian, her scales stern and unyielding. Her form was ethereal and powerful, as if she was carved from pure stone, her body sculpted by the elements of time and the ocean itself. She was grimy and blind, but as dense and wooden as a giant sequoia tree, and as authoritative as a Vedic sage; powerful, noble, afloat, and tolerant, with a capital and provinces, parishes and a Vatican, an orange planet and many angry moons. She was La Madre de Agua, the goddess that never dies. She was La Madre de Agua, an ancient goddess of immense power and wisdom, whose spirit was legendary, said to live forever in the depths of the sea. Her face bore a serene grace that defied time, while her eyes shimmered with an ageless force that commanded awe and respect.

The Madre de Agua was a creature of myth and legend, one that had haunted the depths of the seas since time immemorial. Tales were told of her supernatural strength and imposing stature; but most of all, stories were whispered of her anger and thirst for revenge. For centuries, she had been a symbol of justice and retribution, seeking to punish wickedness wherever it may lurk.

When the seas began to become polluted and abused by humans, La Madre de Agua was stirred from slumber. She emerged from the deep in an oversized form, her colossal body illuminated by a strange glow of electricity. As she made her way through the sewers and canals of Cuba then Mumbai, more tales sprung up claiming she wanted to restore balance to the seas, punishing those who dared to defile her kingdom with their malignant actions.

La Madre de Agua's mission soon attracted a large following. The oppressed, downtrodden masses found comfort in her ideals, gathering at night in cloaked shadows to aid her in whatever way they could. From humble beginnings, she became a figurehead of fear and chaos, striking horror into the hearts of those daring enough to stand against her cause. Her reputation echoed throughout the farthest corners of Mumbai's dark underworld, where even the bravest souls cowered in terror at the mere mention of her otherworldly name.

The sound of Teen Mundi Wali Bai's footsteps echoed like thunder through the alleys of Mumbai. Her voice was like a sharpened blade, slicing through the air with ferocity and anger. She stood tall and confident, her face set in a determined expression. Her eyes were dark but bright with conviction, her hair tied in intricate braids that wrapped around her head like a crown. She wore striking jewelry made from salvaged metals - a testament to her success. Her clothing was simple yet powerful; an array of black and gold fabrics draped over here lithe and strong body. Her skin was cold to the touch, and she carried with her an aura of icy detachment that radiated off of her body. She smelled of sweet jasmine, but beneath it lay an acrid scent of burnt gunpowder and smoke. It carried with it a hint of danger and unrestrained power.

She was Teen Mundi Wali Bai, The Three Headed Lady, and from her humble and troubled beginning in the slums of Mumbai, she emerged with a strength that few people had. Born into poverty and surrounded by violence, she had no choice but to learn how to fight for survival. She used every ounce of her intelligence and fearlessness to build an empire from nothing; a criminal stronghold ruling over the underbelly of the city.

With a heart hardened by years of hardship, she earned an infamous reputation as one of the most fearsome criminals that ever walked the streets. But no one expected that this street-savvy girl would become the queen of Mumbai's crime rings. The fear of her name spread like wildfire across Southwest Mumbai, for she had the power to fell even the mightiest of kingpins. As if it were a rite of passage, Teen Mundi Wali Bai collected two heads as trophies that she would keep with her at all times, cementing her legacy as the Three Headed Lady and striking terror into the hearts of those who spoke out.

The fearsome Teen Mundi Wali Bai reigned as the undisputed queenpin of Mumbai, her reputation for brutality and determination preceding her. She had no mercy for those that would dare cross her or her confidants; a loyalty earned through both loyalty and might. People all throughout the city cowered in fear whenever they heard mention of her name, whispered in hushed tones into quivering ears. Her ascent to power was characterized by calculated moves and crushing blows against anyone who dared challenge her authority. A veritable force of nature, Teen Mundi Wali Bai commanded respect and terror in equal measure.

As La Madre de Agua's influence reached the northwestern district of the city, it seemed as if that day would be fateful for both her and Mundi. Certainly, a fierce clash was expected, yet none anticipated the direction their encounter would take. Amidst their strife, they saw a kindred ambition in each other; a mutual admiration soon took root and their hostilities subsided. But what began as an incongruous partnership has now become a dangerous force against those who dare oppose them.

Teen Mundi Wali Bai eyed La Madre de Agua with a mixture of awe and respect. The creature's tentacles were as thick as tree trunks and waved menacingly in the air. She knew that with her formidable power, her gang could become virtually unstoppable in the Mumbai underworld. When she proposed an alliance between them, she accepted without hesitation. It was an unorthodox partnership; a monstrous sea deity and a feared street boss, but it worked surprisingly well. Mundi gained access to the ocean goddess' unique form of protection and intimidation, while La Madre de Agua had a formidable ground presence with Mundi's criminal empire and fierce gang members at her disposal. Together, they emerged as powerful forces in the city's criminal activities, creating a stronghold over their respective territories.

On the corner of a lonely street in Mumbai, they would meet up in the dead of night and share a plate of vada pav—a humble potato-stuffed deep-fried pastry drenched in sweet and spicy chutney. They'd sip their ginger tea out of glass tumblers and admire the way the steam curled around their faces as they talked about everything and nothing all at once. It had become an unspoken ritual for them, a symbol of their friendship and unique bond.

From the depths of Mumbai's underworld, their unlikely partnership rose like a phoenix, an unstoppable force that kept the city's crime and power in a tight grip. While others reveled in the hustle and bustle of life in Mumbai, these two pushed on relentlessly to defend their hard-earned reign over the streets. Together they forged an alliance that would never be forgotten.

La Madre de Agua and Teen Mundi Wali Bai had joined forces out of necessity, but what started as a strategic alliance soon began to blossom into something far more powerful. They soon found themselves drawn together by an inscrutable force, and the passion between them was undeniable. Their forbidden love defied social conventions, transcending both their monstrous pasts and criminal worlds. But it was a bond that could never be broken; no matter what dangers or disagreements threatened to come between them, their love only deepened with time.

At first, their bond was based on mutual respect and the pragmatic benefits of their partnership. La Madre de Agua's luminescent scales gleamed, and her glistening eyes glared with intensity as she surveyed Mundi's intelligence and fearlessness. Mundi admired the deity's immense power and enigmatic allure, utterly entranced by the way she could command the elements with just a flick of her tentacles. The collaboration of supernatural tentacles and streetwise cunning created an unprecedented force in Mumbai's criminal underworld, and their union seemed unbreakable. Together, they were unstoppable - like a tidal wave crashing against solid stone, or a bolt of lightning striking down from above.

The bond between La Madre de Agua and Mundi grew stronger each passing day. Conversations that once revolved around strategies to protect the village, now filled with dreams of a better future. As they shared laughter and secrets, fears seemed to melt away in La Madre de Agua's presence. Mundi, who was previously feared by all, revealed her vulnerable side to La Madre de Agua, while even the formidable entity softened around Mundi.

Their first tender moments happened during a particularly tumultuous monsoon season. As the rain pounded the city, they found themselves taking shelter in an abandoned building. With the world around them echoing with thunder and lightning, they were drawn together and their gazes met. An electric charge hummed in the air between them as they drew closer and kissed gently. She wrapped her arms around her slender body; she melted into her and ran her hands through her dark hair. The sudden spark of desire sent them reeling as their lips fused once more.

Mundi and La Madre de Agua streaked through the backstreets

of Mumbai with their forbidden love. Danger was never far away, and they had to take their clandestine meetings at dead of night. But La Madre de Agua's loving affection for Mundi softened her terrifying reputation among the street folk of Mumbai. Mundi cherished this newfound protection, listening as she revealed her dreams and ambitions for a brighter future for the city's poor. In return, she vowed to make her vision into reality, no matter what it would cost.

But the course of true love never did run smooth, and their love story was no exception. The very elements that made their partnership so potent in the criminal world also threatened to tear them apart. Rival gang leaders, mystical forces, and the authorities all sought to bring them down.

Desperate and facing overwhelming odds, La Madre de Agua and Mundi Wali Bai clung to each other in a desperate embrace. They had no choice but to rely on each other, but the tension between them was palpable. As they devised strategies to outwit their enemies and protect their criminal empire, there was always a fear that their turbulent emotions would cause a rift between them. Despite their fears, their love for one another only grew deeper, becoming a legend whispered throughout the streets of Mumbai.

Despite the danger and the odds stacked against them, La Madre de Agua and Teen Mundi Wali Bai's love endured, as unbreakable as the underworld empire they ruled. Their passionate love story was a testament to the resilience of love in the most unlikely of circumstances, and it left an indelible mark on the dark and enigmatic streets of Mumbai.

ΔΔΔ

The Jersey Devil

I n the dim glow of the car's headlights, Sarah Montgomery stared at the endless rows of twisted trees that lined the desolate road. She was petite, with shoulder-length dark hair that framed her pale, heart-shaped face. Her green eyes sparkled with intelligence, even as they narrowed in skepticism at the eerie landscape surrounding them. A cautious introvert, she often found solace in books and exploring local legends, though she questioned their validity.

Beside her, Jack Turner maneuvered the car through the narrow path. His tousled brown hair and chiseled features were complemented by piercing blue eyes that never wavered from the road. At 25, he was strong and athletic, his protective instincts always on high alert. Underneath his brave exterior, however, Jack struggled to cope with fear and trauma. It was a side of him he rarely showed, especially not to Sarah, on whom he harbored a secret affection since childhood.

"Did you guys know that the Pine Barrens is home to over a thousand different plant species?" Alex Carter interjected from the backseat, his curly black hair bouncing as he leaned forward eagerly. In contrast to his friends, he was outgoing and charismatic, cracking jokes with ease and regaling tales of folklore that he cherished deeply. The Pine Barrens held a special place in his heart, and his dark brown eyes gleamed with excitement.

The damp shadows of the Pine Barrens seemed to close in around them, ominous and foreboding. The gnarled branches overhead reached out like skeletal fingers, casting eerie patterns on the cracked asphalt below. Despite the darkness, there was an undeniable beauty to the vast expanse of woodland, a primal allure that had drawn the trio into its depths.

"Wow, Alex, I didn't know that," Sarah muttered, her gaze fixed on the shifting shadows outside the window. "I guess there's always something new to learn, even in a place as old as this."

"Exactly!" Alex beamed. "This place is full of surprises. I mean, who knows what could be lurking just beyond our sight?" He wiggled his eyebrows suggestively, eliciting a shiver from Sarah.

"Come on, don't start that again," she chided, trying her best to ignore the unsettling feeling settling in her chest.

"Sorry, couldn't resist." Alex grinned, leaning back in his seat. "But seriously, there's so much history here. It's like stepping into another world."

Jack remained silent, his attention locked on navigating the treacherous road. Though he shared Alex's fascination with the Pine Barrens, his primary concern was ensuring the safety of his friends. The thought of losing Sarah, in particular, filled him with a dread he dared not acknowledge. And so, he swallowed his fear and pressed onward, deeper into the heart of the forest, where fate awaited them all.

"Hey, Jack, why did the ghost go to the bar?" Alex asked, his eyes twinkling with mischief.

"Alright, I'll bite," Jack replied, gripping the steering wheel tightly as he navigated the narrow, winding road through the Pine Barrens. "Why did the ghost go to the bar?"

"For the boos!" Alex exclaimed, laughing at his own joke.

Sarah couldn't help but smile at Alex's antics, her green eyes briefly glancing away from the eerie landscape outside the car window. The dark silhouettes of twisted trees seemed to close in around them, their gnarled branches casting long, spindly shadows that danced and swayed with the car's movement. She found herself drawn to the unsettling beauty of it all, the way the moonlight filtered through the dense canopy above, casting an otherworldly glow on the forest floor.

"Okay, okay, I've got another one," Alex continued, clearly enjoying himself. "What do you call a werewolf with a fever?"

"Give up?" He paused for effect, then announced triumphantly, "A hot dog!"

"Wow, that was terrible," Sarah laughed, shaking her head.

"Terrible? That was comedy gold!" Alex insisted, feigning offense. "I'll have you know, I'm an expert in supernatural humor."

"Is that so?" Sarah asked, raising an eyebrow. "Well, keep 'em coming. It's better than thinking about what might actually be lurking out there." She gestured toward the shadowy forest beyond the car's windows.

"Are you scared?" Alex asked, concern momentarily replacing his playful demeanor.

"Maybe a little," Sarah admitted, averting her gaze from the ominous woods and focusing on the flickering dashboard lights instead. Her heart pounded in her chest, an uneasy feeling creeping into her thoughts despite the lighthearted banter. She berated herself for letting the darkness and Alex's stories get to her.

"Hey, don't worry," Jack reassured her, his blue eyes meeting hers in the rearview mirror for a fleeting moment before returning to the road. "I promise we'll be fine. Just try to relax and enjoy the ride."

"Thanks, Jack," Sarah murmured, grateful for his steadfast presence and silently cursing her own nerves.

"Alright, one more joke to lighten the mood," Alex declared, determined to keep the atmosphere cheerful. "Why did the vampire read the newspaper?"

"Go on," Jack prompted, his eyes never leaving the road ahead.

"Because he heard it had great circulation!" Alex exclaimed, grinning from ear to ear as he reveled in his corny punchline.

The car erupted in laughter, dispelling the tension that had been building within its confines. And though the shadows of the Pine Barrens continued to loom over them, for a brief moment, the fear was forgotten, replaced instead with the warmth of camaraderie and the simple joy of shared laughter.

The laughter in the car faded as suddenly as it had begun, replaced by a silence that seemed to rise up from the depths of the Pine Barrens themselves. Sarah could feel an oppressive stillness settling over them, and she shivered involuntarily. The trees, once swaying gently in the breeze, now stood rigid, as if anticipating some unseen threat.

"Looks like we might be in for some rain," Jack observed, his voice quiet and tinged with concern as he stared at the darkening sky. As if on cue, a heavy drop splattered against the windshield, followed by another, and then a deluge began pouring down from the heavens.

"Damn," Alex muttered, squinting through the rain-streaked window in a futile attempt to make out their surroundings. "It's really coming down."

"Let me turn up the wipers," Jack said, adjusting the controls on the dashboard. The wipers sprang to life, but even their frenetic pace couldn't keep up with the torrential onslaught. Thunder rumbled ominously in the distance, and Sarah felt her stomach twist into knots.

"Maybe we should pull over," she suggested, her voice barely audible above the roar of the storm. "Wait it out?"

"Could be a good idea," Jack agreed, scanning the road for a suitable place to stop. But before he could find one, something slammed into the windshield with enough force to rock the car on its suspension. All three of them gasped in unison, instinctively recoiling from the impact.

"Jesus Christ!" Alex shouted, gripping the door handle so tightly that his knuckles turned white. "What the hell was that?"

"Did we hit something?" Sarah stammered, her heart pounding wildly in her chest.

Jack shook his head, his eyes wide with fear. "No, it...it came from above!"

As if to prove his point, the thing reared up from the hood of the car, revealing its monstrous visage. Glowing red eyes blazed like twin infernos, boring into their very souls as they stared, transfixed by the horror before them. This was no ordinary creature; this was the Jersey Devil itself, a predator born of nightmares and despair.

"Go, Jack! Go!" Alex screamed, terror seizing him by the throat.

"Drive, damn it!" Sarah joined in, her voice high-pitched and frantic. Jack didn't need any further prompting; he slammed his foot down on the accelerator, the car lurching forward as it tore through the storm.

As they raced along the rain-slicked road, Sarah's mind raced with fear, her thoughts a jumble of panic and disbelief. Could they really be under attack by the legendary Jersey Devil? She had heard the stories, but she had never believed they could be true. And yet, there it was, staring them down with those blood-red eyes, a messenger of doom sent to drag them all to hell.

"Keep going, Jack," she whispered, her fingers clutching at the seatbelt that held her in place. "Don't let it catch us. Please."

The stench hit them first, a noxious wave that permeated the car's interior. Sarah gagged as it filled her nostrils, the putrid odor clawing at the back of her throat. It was as if someone had packed a dozen rotting carcasses into a confined space and left them to fester in the sweltering heat.

"Jesus!" Alex choked, his eyes watering as he rolled down the window in a desperate attempt to let in some fresh air. "What is that smell?"

"Never mind the smell!" Jack shouted over the roar of the storm. "We need to lose this thing!"

Sarah could see the panic in his eyes, but she also knew Jack well enough to recognize the determination that lay beneath the surface. He had always been the one they relied on in times of trouble – their rock, their shelter from the storm.

"Swerve!" she yelled, grabbing for the door handle as the car veered sharply to the left. The Jersey Devil clung tenaciously to the hood, its talons screeching against the metal as it fought to maintain its grip. Its wings flapped wildly in the torrential rain, casting eerie shadows on the road ahead.

"Come on, you bastard!" Jack snarled, slamming the wheel to the right and sending the car skidding across the slick pavement. The creature's grip began to falter, its claws tearing through the metal like tissue paper as it struggled to hold on.

"Jack, watch out!" Alex cried, pointing at a sharp bend in the road that loomed up ahead.

"Got it!" Jack responded, his knuckles white as he gripped the steering wheel with all his might.

"Please, please, let this work," Sarah thought, her heart pounding like a jackhammer in her chest. Time seemed to slow down as the car hurtled towards the curve, the Jersey Devil's guttural snarls filling her ears.

"Get off our car, you freak!" Jack yelled, and with a final, decisive jerk of the wheel, he sent the car careening around the bend. The sudden movement was too much for the beast, and it finally lost its grip, tumbling off the hood and disappearing into the darkness.

"Did we lose it?" Alex panted, his face pale as he stared out the window into the storm.

"Keep driving, Jack," Sarah urged, her voice shaking. "Just... just keep going."

As they sped down the rain-soaked road, the only sounds were the pounding of the rain and the ragged breaths of three friends who had just come face to face with the stuff of nightmares. And all the while, Sarah couldn't help but wonder: would they ever truly be able to escape the malevolent gaze of those glowing red eyes?

"Sarah, look out!" Alex screamed as the Jersey Devil, with unexpected agility, leaped onto the roof of the car. The sound of its claws scraping against metal was like nails on a chalkboard, and Sarah could feel the vibrations reverberating throughout the car.

"J-Jack, do something!" she cried, her voice cracking with fear. Her heart thundered in her chest, each beat pounding like a frantic drumbeat echoing through her body. She couldn't tear her gaze away from the blood-red eyes that pierced through the darkness, their sinister glow seeming to bore straight into her soul.

"Get off!" Jack shouted, his own terror mingling with a fierce determination. He jerked the wheel sharply, trying to dislodge the creature from its perch. But the Jersey Devil clung to the roof with supernatural strength, its claws digging deeper into the metal with every swerve and turn.

"Jack, it's not working!" Alex yelled, his usual bravado replaced by sheer panic. He glanced desperately at Sarah, who met his gaze for a brief moment before returning her attention to the monstrous figure atop the car.

"Think, think," Sarah muttered under her breath, her mind racing as she tried to come up with a plan. They needed to find a way to get rid of this thing – and fast. The beast's hellish eyes seemed to burn brighter as it clung tighter to the car, its wicked intentions clear.

"Wait... the bridge!" Jack exclaimed, spotting salvation in the form of a narrow bridge up ahead with low clearance. It was their one chance to shake off the monster, but they'd have to act quickly.

"Gun it, Jack! Gun it!" Sarah shouted, gripping the door handle so tightly her knuckles turned white. Adrenaline coursed through her veins, fueling her desperation.

"Here goes nothing!" Jack cried, flooring the accelerator and sending the car hurtling towards the bridge at breakneck speed. The Jersey Devil let out a blood-curdling screech, its malevolent gaze never leaving them as they raced closer and closer to their potential salvation.

"Come on, come on!" Alex prayed, his eyes squeezed shut in terror. Sarah couldn't help but join him, her heart feeling as though it might burst from her chest.

"Please, please let this work" she thought, barely able to breathe as the car charged towards the bridge, the monstrous creature atop it still refusing to let go.

Jack's hands tightened around the steering wheel, his knuckles turning white. The Jersey Devil's claws scraped against the roof of the car with a sickening screech, like nails on a chalkboard. Jack's heart pounded in his throat, but he refused to let fear overtake him. He needed to get them out of this – alive.

"Damn thing won't let go!" Jack shouted, his voice trembling only slightly. He swerved the car left and right, attempting to dislodge the creature, but it held fast, its claws sinking deeper into the metal. "We have to find a way to get rid of it!"

"Jack, don't you think we're trying?" Sarah cried, her voice wavering as she stared at the monstrous figure above them. The rain continued to pour down, pelting the windshield relentlessly. Thunder cracked, echoing their terror, but it was no match for the sinister howls of the beast that clung to their car.

"Alex, got any ideas?" Jack asked, his desperation growing. It was clear that he would do anything to protect Sarah and himself, even if it meant risking everything. His eyes darted frantically between the road ahead and the rearview mirror, searching for some means of escape.

"Uh... I don't know," Alex stammered, his face pale as a ghost. "Maybe we could... I don't know, man! I've never dealt with a freaking monster before!"

"Neither have I, but now's not the time for panic," Jack snapped, barely able to contain his own rising hysteria. He swallowed hard, fighting to maintain some semblance of control. "We need to focus. We need to outsmart this thing."

"Outsmart it?" Sarah scoffed, tears streaming down her cheeks from the overwhelming mix of emotions. "How the hell do you outsmart something like that?"

"By not giving up!" Jack growled, his jaw set in determination. "There's got to be something we can do."

"Alright, alright," Alex said, taking a deep breath and forcing himself to think. His mind raced, as if searching frantically through every horror movie he'd ever seen for some kind of answer. "Maybe... maybe we could try to blind it? With our high beams or something?"

"Anything's worth a shot," Jack replied, flicking the high beams on full blast. The Jersey Devil screeched again, its eerie wail piercing the stormy air like a knife. But it didn't let go – instead, it seemed even more enraged.

"Jesus, that only made it worse!" Sarah screamed, her hands gripping the seat beneath her as she fought to hold onto some semblance of sanity.

"Okay, bad idea!" Jack admitted, his heart sinking. "We need something else!"

"Jack, I'm scared," Sarah whispered, her voice barely audible above the torrential rain. She looked at him with pleading eyes, seeking some shred of reassurance, some sign that they would make it out alive.

"Me too," Jack confessed, his voice cracking. "But I'm not going to give up, Sarah. We're going to survive this thing, whatever it takes." And in that moment, Jack knew he was no longer just fighting for his own life – he was fighting for hers, too. The girl he'd loved since childhood, whom he'd never had the courage to truly express his feelings for.

"Whatever it takes," Sarah echoed, her fear momentarily overshadowed by the fierce determination Jack's words inspired. Together, they faced the horrifying unknown, united by their will to live and the love that refused to die.

The Jersey Devil's grip on the car tightened, its relentless pursuit emboldened as it seemed to gain strength from their fear. Its claws dug into the metal roof, puncturing the steel and leaving jagged holes in their wake. The creature lunged forward suddenly, its grotesque face pressing against the windshield, baring its teeth in a snarl. Its breath fogged up the glass, filling the air with an acrid stench that burned their nostrils and made Alex gag.

"Jack, do something!" Sarah cried, her voice strained and raw. "It's getting worse!"

"Alright, alright," Jack muttered, his knuckles white on the steering wheel. His mind raced, sifting through a whirlwind of thoughts and panic, desperately searching for a solution. He knew he had to stay focused, not just for himself, but for Sarah and Alex too. Failure was not an option.

"Look at this thing!" Alex shouted, pointing to a part of the map that had been hastily stuffed in the glove compartment. "There's a bridge marked here, just up ahead! Maybe we can use it to knock this bastard off!"

"Let me see!" Jack grabbed the map, his eyes scanning the crude lines and symbols. Sure enough, there it was – a bridge spanning a narrow river, barely wide enough for a single vehicle. Jack couldn't be certain, but he guessed the clearance might be low enough to dislodge the beast clinging to their car.

"Okay," Jack said, steeling himself for what lay ahead. "We're going for it." He glanced at Sarah, their eyes locking in a silent exchange of trust and determination. They'd come this far; they wouldn't back down now.

"Be careful," she whispered, her breath hitching in her throat.

"Always am," Jack replied, flashing her a half-smile that didn't quite reach his eyes. He focused on the road, the rain pounding against the windshield like a relentless drumbeat, drowning out all other sounds.

"Here it comes!" Alex yelled, pointing to the looming structure just visible through the dark and stormy night. "Floor it!"

"Alright, hold on!" Jack shouted, pressing the accelerator to the floor. The car's engine roared in response, launching them forward at breakneck speed. As they approached the bridge, Jack could see that it was even narrower than the map had suggested – only a few feet of clearance on either side. His heart raced, adrenaline coursing through his veins as he realized just how dangerous this maneuver would be.

"God, Jack," Sarah breathed, her eyes wide with terror. "Are you sure about this?"

"Trust me," Jack replied, his voice steadier than he felt. Deep down, he knew there was no guarantee that any of them would survive this desperate gambit. But if they didn't try, the Jersey Devil would surely pick them off one by one.

"Okay," Sarah whispered, gripping his hand tightly. "We trust you."

"Here goes nothing," Jack muttered, steeling himself for the impact.

The Jersey Devil's relentless pursuit was a nightmare made flesh, its grotesque form mirrored in the bloodshot eyes of the terror-stricken passengers. The creature's talons dug into the roof of the car, metal screeching and groaning beneath its monstrous grip. Its wings flapped violently, propelling it forward with unnatural speed and strength.

"Look!" Alex cried out, his voice cracking under the strain. "Up ahead...a bridge!"

Jack's gaze darted toward the structure looming in the distance. He could see it now, barely visible through the storm – a narrow crossing, its low clearance creating a tight squeeze that might just prove to be their salvation. He glanced at Sarah, her beautiful face pale and drawn as she stared back at him, her breath hitching in her throat.

"Can you make it?" she whispered, her fingers tightening around his arm.

"Always can," Jack replied, flashing her a half-smile that didn't quite reach his eyes. He focused on the road, the rain pounding against the windshield like a relentless drumbeat, drowning out all other sounds.

"Here it comes!" Alex yelled, pointing to the looming structure just visible through the dark and stormy night. "Floor it!"

"Alright, hold on!" Jack shouted, pressing the accelerator to the floor. The car's engine roared in response, launching them forward at breakneck speed. As they approached the bridge, Jack could see that it was even narrower than the map had suggested – only a few feet of clearance on either side. His heart raced, adrenaline coursing through his veins as he realized just how dangerous this maneuver would be.

"God, Jack," Sarah breathed, her eyes wide with terror. "Are you sure about this?"

"Trust me," Jack replied, his voice steadier than he felt. Deep down, he knew there was no guarantee that any of them would survive this desperate gambit. But if they didn't try, the Jersey Devil would surely pick them off one by one.

"Okay," Sarah whispered, gripping his hand tightly. "We trust you."

"Here goes nothing," Jack muttered, steeling himself for the impact.

The car's tires screeched as it skidded to a halt, the rain-slicked road gleaming darkly under the ominous storm clouds above. Sarah peered out of the window, her green eyes wide with shock, heart pounding in her chest like a jackhammer. The creature they'd just struck had been hurled from the roof of their vehicle into the turbulent waters of the river below.

"Jesus Christ," Jack muttered beside her, hands still gripping the steering wheel so tightly that his knuckles had turned bone white.

"Was that...?" Sarah began, her voice trembling. She couldn't even bring herself to say it. The Jersey Devil? No, it couldn't be. It was just some poor, misshapen animal caught out in the storm. That was all. Right?

"Probably just a coincidence," she said aloud, more to reassure herself than anything else. "An animal spooked by the storm."

"Coincidence?" Jack shot her an incredulous look. "You saw that thing, Sarah! That was no ordinary animal. It was... I don't know what it was."

"Look, we're all on edge because of the stories we've heard about the Pine Barrens," she reasoned, trying to remain calm despite her racing pulse. "It's easy for our minds to play tricks on us."

"Tricks?" Jack shook his head, disbelief etched across his face. "That thing was on our car, Sarah. It attacked us!"

"Maybe it was... I don't know, a deformed deer or something." She knew how ridiculous it sounded, but she clung to the idea anyway.

Anything to banish the cold dread gnawing at the pit of her stomach.

"Deer don't have wings," Jack retorted, his voice tinged with frustration. "Or glowing red eyes."

"Okay, fine," she snapped, her fear giving way to irritation at his insistence. "But that doesn't mean it was the Jersey Devil. That's just a legend."

"Is it?" Jack looked back out into the rain, his eyes searching for any sign of the creature they'd struck. "I'm not so sure anymore."

"Jack, please." She reached over and touched his arm, trying to ground him in reality. "We're both scared and confused, but jumping to conclusions won't help us."

"Maybe not," he conceded, finally turning the key to start the engine once more. "But we can't just pretend nothing happened. We need to get out of here. Now."

"Agreed," she whispered, feeling that same twisting knot of fear return to her belly. It didn't matter whether the creature they'd encountered was the legendary Jersey Devil or just some unfortunate animal caught in their headlights - what mattered was putting as much distance between themselves and the Pine Barrens as possible.

As the car pulled away from the scene, Sarah couldn't shake the feeling that they were being watched. The storm continued to rage overhead, casting eerie shadows that seemed to dance and twist in the darkness, leaving them with nothing but questions, doubts, and a lingering sense of dread.

Rain lashed against the windshield, blurring the already dark and twisted road. The wipers struggled to keep up, leaving streaks of water behind in their wake. In the backseat, Alex leaned forward, his dark eyes gleaming with curiosity.

"Guys, can you imagine if it really was the Jersey Devil?" he asked, unable to contain his excitement. "I mean, we've all heard the stories, but to actually encounter it? That would be incredible!"

"Let's not get carried away, Alex," Jack said, gripping the steering wheel tightly as he navigated the treacherous path before them. "Sarah has a point. We don't know what that thing was."

"Of course!" Alex agreed, nodding vigorously. "But it's still fascinating to think about, isn't it?" He looked over at Sarah, whose green eyes were fixed on the road ahead. "You like exploring local legends, right? This could be something big."

"Alex, now is not the time," Sarah snapped, her voice tense. She turned to look at him, her face pale and drawn. "We need to focus on getting out of these woods, not entertaining fantasies."

"Hey, I'm just trying to lighten the mood," Alex said defensively, holding his hands up in surrender. "Besides, I thought you'd be interested in digging deeper into this mystery."

"Normally, yes," she admitted, her gaze dropping to her lap. "But right now, all I want is to put as much distance between us and... whatever that was."

"Fine," Alex huffed, leaning back in his seat. "But when we get home, I fully intend to do some research. There's got to be more to this story."

"Look, Alex—" Jack started, but Sarah cut him off.

"Let him have his fun," she sighed, rubbing her temples. "As long as we're safe and away from here, he can research whatever he wants."

"Exactly!" Alex said triumphantly, his face lighting up with enthusiasm. "And who knows? Maybe we'll find something that'll finally prove the existence of the Jersey Devil once and for all!"

"Or maybe we'll just have a good laugh at some old myths," Jack countered, trying to keep the mood light. In the back of his mind, however, his own doubts lingered, gnawing at him like a persistent itch. He shivered, feeling the weight of the dark forest pressing in on them from all sides.

"Whatever the case," Sarah murmured, staring out into the rain-soaked night, "let's just make it through tonight in one piece, okay?"

"Agreed," Jack and Alex said in unison, their voices barely audible above the pounding of the rain.

The car continued down the winding road, the three friends silent as they grappled with their own thoughts and fears. The storm outside raged on, casting a pall over the night, leaving them with an unsettling sense that the shadows held secrets best left undiscovered.

The rain drummed a relentless rhythm on the roof of the car, each drop hammering down like a nail into their already frayed nerves. Alex gripped the steering wheel tightly, his knuckles white as he squinted through the windshield, trying to discern the road ahead from the dark, impenetrable night.

"Jesus," Sarah whispered, her voice trembling despite her attempt at bravado. "I can't believe that actually happened. I mean, what the hell was that thing?"

"Look, it was probably just some kind of animal that we didn't recognize," Jack offered, though the wavering in his voice betrayed his own lingering fear. He stared out the window, watching the trees whip past them as the wind howled like a pack of ravenous wolves.

"An animal that almost ripped our car apart?" Alex countered, his grip on the wheel never relaxing. "That thing had wings, man. And those eyes - they were glowing red!"

"Maybe it was just a trick of the light," Sarah suggested, but her words held little conviction. She shuddered, drawing her knees up to her chest and wrapping her arms around herself as if to ward off the chill that had settled over them all.

"Whatever it was, we need to get as far away from here as possible," Jack said, his eyes meeting Alex's in the rearview mirror. "Let's just put this whole night behind us."

"Agreed," Alex replied, nodding his head resolutely. There would be time for investigation later; right now, the only thing that mattered was putting distance between them and whatever it was that had attacked them.

"Hey, uh, let's not tell anyone about this, okay?" Sarah suggested, her eyes darting nervously between her friends. "People will think we're crazy or something."

"Fine by me," Jack said, nodding his agreement. "I'd prefer to forget this whole thing ever happened, anyway."

"Alright, deal," Alex muttered, mostly to himself, as he pressed down on the accelerator. His heart raced with a mix of adrenaline and lingering terror, but he knew they had to get out of the Pine Barrens before anything else could happen.

As the car sped away from the scene of their encounter, the friends exchanged furtive glances, each haunted by the images of the night's events that replayed in their minds like a horror film on an endless loop. The rain poured down around them, seeming to wash away any evidence of the nightmare they had just escaped, but the memory clung to them like wet clothes, heavy and cold.

"Let's just hope we're really done with that thing," Sarah murmured, her voice barely audible above the relentless storm.

"Me too," Alex whispered, swallowing hard as he willed his hands to stop shaking. With every mile they put between themselves and the Pine Barrens, the weight of what they had experienced seemed to lift, bit by agonizing bit. But one question still burned in the back of their minds, unspoken yet impossible to ignore: would they ever truly be free of the terror they had witnessed?

The wind howled through the trees, their gnarled branches reaching out like skeletal fingers in the darkness. The car's headlights pierced through the veil of rain, casting eerie shadows that danced and swayed along the deserted road. Alex gripped the steering wheel, knuckles white, as his foot pressed harder on the accelerator. Sarah and Jack sat silently, their uneasy breathing barely audible above the storm's tumultuous growl.

"Damn," Jack muttered, staring at the water streaming down the window. "It's like the heavens are crying for us."

"More like laughing," Sarah replied, her voice laced with bitterness. She twisted a loose strand of hair around her finger and yanked it harshly, as if punishing herself for her earlier skepticism. "We should've listened to those stories. Instead, we thought we were invincible."

"None of us could have known," Alex said, trying to offer some comfort. His mind churned with memories of the Jersey Devil's grotesque form and the terror in its red eyes. He fought the urge to glance in the rearview mirror, afraid that he'd see the creature following them. "We made it out alive. That's what matters."

"Is it?" Sarah asked, her tone sardonic. "You saw that thing, Alex. It isn't human or animal. We can't just leave it behind and pretend nothing happened."

"Getting ourselves killed won't help either," Jack chimed in, rubbing his temple where a throbbing headache had taken root. "We need to regroup and make a plan. If we're going to do something about it, we need to be smart."

"Jack's right," Alex agreed, glancing at him with a nod. As much as he wanted to learn more about the Jersey Devil, he couldn't let his curiosity dictate their actions. "Let's put some distance between us and this place, then we can figure out what to do."

"Fine," Sarah grumbled, crossing her arms over her chest. "But I won't be able to sleep until that thing is gone. For good."

"None of us will," Jack added, his voice tight with suppressed emotion.

As they continued to drive away from the Pine Barrens, the storm seemed to intensify, as if nature itself were mourning the terror that had been unleashed upon it. Lightning cracked across the sky, illuminating the twisted landscape in flashes of stark, cold light, and the thunder rumbled like a growl from some angry beast.

"Keep going," Sarah urged, her voice barely audible above the cacophony. "Don't stop for anything."

"Trust me," Alex replied, his own voice wavering, "I have no intention of stopping." His thoughts were a whirlwind of fear and uncertainty, but one thing was clear: they couldn't let the Jersey Devil continue its reign of terror. They had to find a way to end it, once and for all.

The windshield wipers slashed back and forth, fighting a losing battle against the relentless downpour. Rivulets of rainwater streaked across the glass, blurring the world outside into a hazy, indistinct nightmare. The oppressive silence within the car weighed heavily upon them, each friend lost in their own private hell, replaying the horror they had just survived.

"Christ," Jack muttered, his knuckles white as he gripped the steering wheel. His eyes flitted from the road to the rearview mirror, as if expecting the Jersey Devil's monstrous visage to reappear at any moment.

"Keep it together," Sarah whispered, her voice trembling with unspoken fear. She stared out the passenger window, watching the shadows of twisted, gnarled trees looming over them like grasping hands.

"Guys, we need to talk about this," Alex began, his voice barely audible above the roar of the storm. He shifted uncomfortably in the backseat, his eyes darting from one friend to the other, searching for some semblance of shared understanding. "What are we going to do?"

Jack swallowed hard, his Adam's apple bobbing as he struggled to find the words. "We... we need to figure out how to stop it. That thing... it's not going to just stop on its own."

"Stop it?" Sarah scoffed, bitterness lacing her tone. "How the hell are we supposed to stop something like that?"

"Research," Alex suggested, his voice gaining strength as he clung to the idea. "Maybe there's a way to kill it. Or... or banish it, or something."

"Right," Jack agreed, nodding tersely. "There's got to be something. A weakness. A vulnerability. Something we can use against it."

"Fine," Sarah relented, though her features remained tight with tension. "But let's do it far away from here. I don't want to spend one more minute in these godforsaken woods."

"Agreed," Jack and Alex said in unison, their voices tinged with a grim determination that belied the terror gnawing at their insides.

The night was oppressive, a palpable darkness that seemed to close in around the car as it sped down the desolate highway. Thick fog rolled across the asphalt, obscuring the view ahead and swallowing the headlights' beams.

"Slow down, Jack!" Sarah's breathless plea cut through the nervous chatter in the vehicle. "You're gonna get us killed!"

"Relax, Sarah," Jack replied, his knuckles white on the steering wheel. "I've got this."

The words had barely left his lips when it happened. An enormous winged figure burst from the fog, its red eyes blazing like hot coals. The Jersey Devil had returned.

"Jesus Christ!" Jack screamed, swerving the car violently in a desperate attempt to avoid the creature. But it was too late. With a bone-shattering impact, the Jersey Devil slammed into the side of the vehicle, sending it careening off the road.

"Jack!" Sarah shrieked, her voice cracking with terror as the car began to roll.

"Alex!" Jack shouted, reaching out instinctively for his friend in the passenger seat. But his hand met only empty air as the world inside the car became a cacophony of noise and motion.

"Brace yourselves!" he managed to choke out, but it was futile advice. Metal screamed against metal as the car tumbled end over end, glass shattering in a thousand brilliant shards. The violent impact threw them around the cab like rag dolls, their bodies colliding with every surface, helpless to stop the devastating crash.

"Stop! God, please!" Sarah cried out, her hands gripping the backseat cushion so tightly her knuckles turned ghostly pale. Her mind raced with panicked thoughts: This can't be happening. We have to survive this. Please, don't let it end like this!

But the car continued to flip, the brutal force threatening to tear it apart. And as the chaos of destruction raged around them, the Jersey Devil's malevolent eyes never left their prey.

The car finally came to a jarring halt, metallic groans and the tinkle of broken glass echoing through the night. Alex's breaths were ragged, blood trickling down the side of his face from a deep gash at his hairline. He blinked, dazed, trying to process what had just happened.

"Jack... Sarah..." he croaked, his voice barely audible over the ringing in his ears. "You guys okay?"

"Alex, look out!" Jack screamed, his eyes widening in terror as the Jersey Devil descended upon the wreckage.

Time seemed to slow down as the creature's talons tore through the shattered window, grasping at Alex with an eerie precision. His heart pounded in his chest, adrenaline surging through his veins – but there was no escape. The Jersey Devil's claws sank into his flesh, ripping into his shoulder like red-hot knives.

"NO!" he shrieked, the searing pain overwhelming him. Panic bubbled up inside his mind, blurring the edges of his vision. *I don't want to die. Not like this.*

"Get away from him, you bastard!" Jack snarled, lashing out with a desperate ferocity as he tried to fend off the beast. But the Jersey Devil was relentless, fueled by an insatiable hunger that could not be denied.

"Help me!" Alex sobbed, reaching out for his friend, but there was nothing Jack could do. The creature ripped into him again and again, its powerful jaws crunching through bone and sinew like paper, tearing him apart piece by piece.

"Please, don't," Jack pleaded, his voice cracking with helplessness. The horror of watching his best friend being devoured alive threatened to break him, but he couldn't tear his eyes away. *Why can't I save him?* he thought, the weight of guilt crushing him even as the beast consumed Alex before his eyes.

"Jack... it hurts..." Alex whispered, blood bubbling from his lips as he drew a final, shuddering breath.

"Alex!" Jack screamed, but it was too late. The Jersey Devil had claimed its first victim – and it wasn't done yet.

The creature turned its attention to Jack, its blood-smeared maw stretching into an unnerving grin. Its red eyes seemed to pierce straight into his soul, a promise of torment that sent icy tendrils of fear down his spine.

"Stay back!" he shouted, his hands shaking as he tried to fend off the Jersey Devil's advance. But the creature's powerful limbs easily overpowered him, pinning him down with a crushing force that left him gasping for breath.

"Please... don't," he choked out, knowing the words were useless even as they left his lips. The monster closed in on him, its fetid breath washing over him like a wave of decay. As the darkness of death enveloped him, all Jack could think about was Sarah – and how he would never get the chance to tell her how much he loved her.

Sarah's heart hammered in her chest, her green eyes wide with terror as she watched the monstrous creature tear into Alex. She could hear his bones crunch and snap beneath the beast's claws, each horrifying sound burrowing deep into her memory. A scream tore through her throat, raw and helpless.

"Stop!" she cried out, tears streaming down her face. "Please, just stop!"

But the Jersey Devil showed no mercy. It continued to rip Alex apart until there was nothing left but a blood-soaked ruin of flesh and gore.

"Jack!" Sarah pleaded, desperation welling up inside her. Jack, her secret crush, the man who held her heart. If anyone could save them, it would be him.

"Sarah, stay back!" Jack yelled, his voice trembling with fear. He lunged at the creature, fists swinging, but to no avail. The Jersey Devil snatched him up, its claws sinking into his flesh like hot knives.

"Help me!" Jack screamed, his blue eyes wild with pain and terror. Sarah tried to reach for him, but she knew in her heart that there was nothing she could do. She was powerless against this monstrosity, forced to watch as her friends were devoured before her very eyes.

The Jersey Devil tossed Jack's mangled body aside, spitting out his remains like a discarded toy. Its bloodshot eyes fixed on Sarah, its malevolence palpable as it bared its jagged teeth.

"Wh-what do you want from us?" Sarah stuttered, her breath hitching in her throat. The creature didn't answer – instead, it began to feed her the grisly remnants of her friends, shoving the pieces into her mouth with sadistic glee.

"Please... don't make me do this," she choked out between sobs, her stomach roiling with revulsion. The taste of death and despair filled her mouth, a nauseating reminder of what had befallen her loved ones.

"God... why is this happening?" Sarah's mind raced with questions, but there were no answers. Only the cruel laughter of the Jersey Devil as it continued its gruesome feast.

"Fight, Sarah," she told herself, even as her body trembled with fear. "You have to fight." But how could she stand against such an unstoppable force of evil? The odds seemed insurmountable – and yet, she knew that giving in meant certain death.

"Get away from me!" Sarah screamed, summoning the last of her strength to push the vile creature away. But it was not enough. The Jersey Devil bore down on her, its twisted smile a promise of further torment.

The car's shattered windows gleamed like a hundred sinister eyes, taunting Sarah as she struggled to free herself. Her fingers trembled in terror, unable to grasp the frayed seatbelt that held her prisoner. She gagged at the acrid stench of blood and bile that filled the air, the remnants of Jack's violent end.

"Please," she whispered, voice quivering with desperation. "Please,

God, no."

The Jersey Devil loomed closer, its twisted form casting an elongated shadow over her trembling body. The creature's red eyes burned like embers, its clawed hand reaching for her, dripping with gore from her friends. Sarah's heart pounded so furiously she could feel it reverberating through her bones.

"Get away!" she screamed, kicking out wildly, her feet connecting with the creature's leathery hide. It barely flinched, and her attempts to fight back only seemed to amuse it further.

"Sarah, you have to do something. Think!" she implored herself, even as the reality of her situation threatened to crush her spirit entirely.

"Le-leave me alone!" she gasped, pulling at the door handle in a last-ditch attempt to escape. But the mangled metal refused to budge, leaving Sarah trapped with the relentless monster.

"Pathetic human," the Jersey Devil hissed, its fetid breath washing over her face like a wave of rancid decay. "You cannot escape your fate."

"No!" Sarah cried, tears streaming down her cheeks even as she continued to claw at the door, her nails breaking and bleeding. "You can't have me! I won't let you!"

"Your defiance is futile," it snarled, its grotesque features contorted into a grin of pure malice.

In that moment, the creature lunged forward, its massive bulk slamming into Sarah with the force of a wrecking ball. The air was driven from her lungs, and her vision blurred as pain exploded through her body.

"Sarah!" she screamed inside her head, feeling her bones splinter beneath the monstrous weight. "Don't give up! Fight!"

But it was too late – the Jersey Devil's crushing embrace had sealed her fate. As her ribs snapped like dry twigs and her spine crumpled under the pressure, Sarah's final thoughts were haunted by the memories of those she loved and the life she would never have the chance to live.

"Jack," she whispered, her voice barely audible above the sound of her own body breaking. "I'm so sorry."

And then, mercifully, the darkness swallowed her whole.

The Jersey Devil's grotesque maw twisted into a perverse smile as it gazed down at Sarah's lifeless body, her once-vibrant green eyes now glazed over with the stillness of death. It reached out with one gnarled claw and tore away the tatters of her clothing, exposing the pale flesh beneath.

"Such tender morsels," it hissed, its voice a sickly-sweet blend of mockery and hunger. "Your defiance only served to make your demise all the more delectable."

Sarah could no longer hear its taunts, but if she had, her heart would have burned with rage at the beast's cruel words. She had fought so hard, tried so desperately to cling to life, and yet in the end, it had all been for naught.

"Please," she might have whispered, her spirit weeping for the life that had been stolen from her. "Don't let this be the end."

But the Jersey Devil took no heed of the silent pleas, instead lowering its head to sink its teeth into the soft flesh of Sarah's breasts. The sound of ripping skin and tearing muscle filled the air, punctuated by the creature's guttural growls of satisfaction. It reveled in the carnage, its monstrous appetite driving it to consume every last scrap of her body.

As it fed, the blood-soaked scene around it seemed to fade into insignificance, leaving only the macabre tableau of predator and prey. This was its domain, its kingdom of fear and pain, and there was no place here for mercy or hope.

At last, when nothing remained of the young woman but a few ragged scraps of flesh and bone, the Jersey Devil raised its head and howled its triumph to the night sky. Its victory was complete, its hunger sated, and it knew that its legend would live on through the terror it inspired in the hearts of those who dared to venture into its territory.

"Remember me," it whispered to the wind, its words carried away on the cold breeze. "Fear me... and despair."

With a powerful beat of its leathery wings, the Jersey Devil took to the air, leaving behind the grisly remains of its feast. As it disappeared into the darkness, the world seemed to hold its breath, as if mourning the loss of innocence that had been so brutally snuffed out.

"Forgive me, Sarah," Jack's spirit might have called after her, his own anguish echoing through the void between life and death. "I tried to save you... I'm so sorry..."

But there would be no solace for the dead tonight, only the cold embrace of oblivion and the terrible knowledge that their suffering had only served to fuel the legend of the Jersey Devil. And as the night wore on, the shadows grew darker, and the silence deepened, one truth remained:

There was no escaping the monster that lurked within the Pine Barrens.

ΔΔΔ

About The Author
The Craptitude

"The Craptitude," a pen name cloaked in mystery and obscurity, is a master of the macabre and a weaver of eerie tales that captivate the darkest corners of the imagination. Known for their unparalleled ability to invoke spine-tingling fear, The Craptitude is an enigmatic figure, and little is known about their identity.